Inside, her mind spun. It was like having a color wheel for a brain. When it slowed down, things were separate, like primary colors: *I have a mother and father . . . I have a childhood . . . I was not kidnapped . . . kidnapping means bad people . . . I don't know any bad people . . . therefore I am making this up.*

But when her mind speeded up, the colors blended dizzily. *That is me on there. I, Janie Johnson; I was kidnapped.*

But it could not be.

The facts did not compute.

She tried to climb outside her mind and go where her body was: sitting neatly at a desk, neatly taking notes.

It was like crawling on glass. No matter how firmly she resolved not to think such stupid things, she thought them. She slithered backward into her mind.

Other Bantam Starfire Books you will enjoy

The Face on the Milk Carton

CAROLINE B. COONEY

BANTAM BOOKS
New York • Toronto • London • Sydney • Auckland

To my mother,
Martha Willerton Bruce,
and my father,
Dexter Mitchell Bruce

RL 6, age 10 and up

THE FACE ON THE MILK CARTON
A Bantam Book
Bantam hardcover edition / March 1990
Bantam paperback edition / May 1991

The
Face
on the
Milk
Carton

CHAPTER
1

Janie finished her essay.

She never knew what grade she would get in Mr. Brylowe's English class. Whenever she joked, he wanted the essay serious. Whenever she was serious, he had intended the essay to be light-hearted.

It was October.

Outdoors throbbed with autumn. She could feel the pulse of the deep-blue skies. With every leaf wrenched off its twig and whirled by the wind, Janie felt a tug. She felt like driving for hours; taking any road at all; just going.

Actually Janie was only fifteen and had barely started driving lessons. She was having driving fantasies because of dinner last night.

Her parents—as always—had taken opposite sides. Setting themselves up like a debate team, her mother and father would argue until some invisible marital timer rang. Then they would come to terms, rushing to meet in the middle. Until last night her mother had said Janie could begin driving while her father said she could not. "She's just a baby," said her father, in the infuriating, affectionate way of fathers.

"She's *old*," said Janie's mother lightly. "Practically a woman. A sophomore in high school."

"I hate when that happens," her father grumbled. "I like my little girl to stay little. I'm against all this growing up." He wound some of Janie's hair around his wrist.

Janie had fabulous hair: a wild, chaotic mane of red curls glinting gold. People always commented on it. As her best friend, Sarah-Charlotte, said, "Janie, that is *serious* hair."

"I guess you've grown up anyway, Janie," said her father reluctantly. "Even with all the bricks I put on your head to keep you little. Okay, I give in. You can drive."

In English, Janie smiled to herself. Her father was an accountant who in the fall had time to coach the middle-school soccer teams. Today after school he'd have a practice, or a game, but when he came home—they'd go driving!

She wrote her name on her essay.

She had gradually changed her name. "Jane" was too dull. Last year she'd added a "y," becoming Jayne, which had more personality and was sexier. To her last name—Johnson—she'd added a "t," and later an "e" at the end, so now she was Jayne Johnstone.

Her best friends—Sarah-Charlotte Sherwood and Adair O'Dell—had wonderful, tongue-twisting, memorable names. Why, with the last name Johnson (hardly a name at all; more like a page out of the phone book) had her parents chosen "Jane"? They could have named her Scarlett, or Allegra. Perhaps Roxanne.

Now she took the "h" out of Johnston and added a second "y" to Jayne.

Jayyne Jonstone. It looked like the name you would have if you designed sequined gowns for a living, or pointed to prizes on television quiz shows.

"Earth to Janie," said Mr. Brylowe.

She blushed, wondering how many times he had called her.

"The rest of us are reading our essays aloud, Janie," said Mr. Brylowe. "We'd like to issue an invitation for you to join us."

She blushed so hotly she had to put her hands over her cheeks.

"Don't do that," said Pete. "You're cute when your face matches your hair."

Immediately, the back row of boys went into barbershop singing, hands on hearts, invisible straw hats flung into the air. "Once in love with Janie," they sang.

Janie had never had a boyfriend. She was always asked to dances, was always with a crowd—but no boy had actually said *I want to be with you and you alone.*

Mr. Brylowe told Janie to read her essay aloud.

The blush faded. She felt white and sick. She hated standing up in class. Hated hearing her voice all alone in the quiet of the room.

The bell rang.

English was a split period: they had lunch in

the middle and came back for more class. Never had lunch come at such an appropriate moment. Perhaps she would write a better essay during the twenty-seven minutes of lunch.

Certainly it wasn't going to take Janie long to eat. They had recently discovered she had a lactose intolerance. This was a splashy way of saying she had stomachaches when she drank milk. "No more ice cream, no more milk" was the medical/parental decree.

However, peanut butter sandwiches (which she had in her bag lunch) required milk. I am so sick of fruit juice, Janie thought. I want milk.

She had been eating since the school year began with Pete, Adair, Sarah-Charlotte, Jason, and Katrina.

She loved all their names.

Her last-year's daydream—before a driver's license absorbed all daydream time—had been about her own future family. She couldn't picture her husband-to-be, but she could see her children perfectly: two beautiful little girls, and she would name them Denim and Lace. She used to think about Denim and Lace all the time. Shopping at the mall with Sarah-Charlotte, she'd go into all the shoe stores to play with the little teeny sneakers for newborns, and think of all the pretty clothes she'd buy one day for Denim and Lace.

Now she knew those names were nauseating, and if she did name her daughters Denim and Lace, there'd probably be a divorce, and her husband would get custody on the grounds anybody who chose those names was unfit. She'd have to name them something sensible, like Emily and Margaret.

Peter, Adair, Sarah-Charlotte, Jason, Katrina, and Janie went in a mob down the wide stairs, through the wide halls, and into the far-too-small cafeteria. The kids complained about the architecture of the school (all that space dedicated to passing periods and hardly any to lunch), but they loved being crammed in, filching each other's potato chips, telling secrets they wanted everybody to overhear, passing notes to be snatched up by the boy you hoped would snatch them, and sending the people on the outside of the crush to get you a second milk.

Everybody but Janie Johnson got milk: cardboard cartons so small you needed at least three, but the lunch ladies would never let you. Janie was envious. Those luckies are swigging down nice thick white milk, she thought, and I'm stuck with cranberry juice.

"Okay," said Sarah-Charlotte. Sarah-Charlotte would not bother with you if you tried to abbreviate her name. Last year she had reached a standoff with a teacher who insisted on calling her Sarah. Sarah-Charlotte glared at him silently for months until he began calling her Miss Sherwood, which let them both win. "Okay, who's been kidnapped this time?" said Sarah-Charlotte wearily, as if jaded with the vast number of kidnappings in the world. Sarah-Charlotte patted her white-blond hair, which was as neat as if she had cut it out of a magazine and pasted it onto her head. Janie, whose mass of hair was never the same

5

two minutes in a row, and whose face could be difficult to find beneath the red tangles, never figured out how Sarah-Charlotte kept her hair so neat. "I have approximately five hundred thousand fewer hairs than you do," Sarah-Charlotte explained once.

Everybody turned the milk cartons over to see who had been kidnapped. The local dairy put pictures of stolen children on the back of the carton. Every few weeks there was a new child.

"I don't know how you're supposed to recognize somebody who was three years old when she got taken from a shopping center in New Jersey, and that was nearly a dozen years ago," said Adair. "It's ridiculous." Adair was as sleek and smooth as her name; even her dark hair matched: unruffled and gleaming like a seal out of water.

Janie sipped juice from a cardboard packet and pretended it was milk. Across the cafeteria Reeve waved. Reeve lived next door. He was a senior. Reeve never did homework. It was his life ambition to get in the *Guinness Book of World Records*, and the only thing he had a stab at was the "Never Did His Homework Once but Still Got the Occasional B Plus" listing.

Reeve had gotten the occasional B plus, but he had also gotten a lot of D's and F's. News came from the Academic Office that unless Reeve shaped up, he would not graduate with his class.

His two older sisters and one older brother had gone to spectacular colleges—Cornell, Princeton, and Stanford. They were mortified by Reeve's failures and came home weekends to tell him so.

Reeve had ceased to speak to his entire family. In fact, he stomped away and had supper at Janie's so often that Janie's mother had said last night, "I'm thinking of charging your parents a meal fee."

Reeve did not laugh. In a strangled voice he said, "I'm sorry. I won't come again."

Janie's father punched him, the way, if it had been Janie, he would have hugged. Jabbing Reeve in the gut, her father said, "Meals here, bed there, Reeve. Someday we'll collect our debt."

"Yeah, when I'm a plumber," said Reeve gloomily, "you'll let me clean your drains."

"Now, Reeve. Just start studying, pull those grades up, and—" Her father broke off. "Right," he said, punching Reeve again. "In this house we won't discuss it. Here. Have a brownie and some ice cream."

It was such a trespass on Reeve, that everybody knew the details. Whatever Reeve kept secret, his mother told Janie's mother anyway. Reeve felt cramped by the intimacy of his life: he had always lived in this town, always gone to this school. I want to live in a city, he'd said last night, and be anonymous.

Ruefully Janie thought her name would give her a pretty good start if she wanted to go anonymous.

Sarah-Charlotte was hoping Reeve would ask Janie out. Sarah-Charlotte was not interested in getting her driver's license; she was interested in having a steady boyfriend, who had to be tall, handsome, muscular, smart, courteous, and rich. Reeve was all but one.

"And if Reeve doesn't ask you out," was Sarah-Charlotte's theory, "maybe his friends will."

Janie did not think the boy next door ever came through in real life. Nor would any of Reeve's friends ask her out. Last year's seniors had dated lots of younger girls. This year's seniors seemed annoyed that they had to be in the same building. And Janie felt younger than her age: she had grown later, and grown less. While Adair and Sarah-Charlotte were busy becoming sophisticated and articulate, Janie remained small. Her mother said she was cute. Janie loathed that word. Cute was for toddlers and kittens. Boys didn't date cute little girls. They dated streamlined, impressive women like Sarah-Charlotte and Adair.

Besides, how would she date?

Her parents didn't even let her go to the shopping mall alone. They'd never let her date. Alone with a boy? Hah. Not likely.

Janie waved back at Reeve and he turned to his friends, duty done. If he knew I'm really Jayyne Jonstone, she thought, would he do more than wave?

She felt curiously heavy: like the difference between whole milk and skim. Through the cafeteria windows the sun gleamed, filling the school with golden shafts in which dust swirled.

On her left—so close he was nearly in her lap—Pete drank his milk in one long swig and crushed the carton in his hand. The boys loved doing that.

If they had a soda, they stamped the can under their feet and looked proudly at the flat aluminum.

"My mother says none of them are really kidnapped anyhow," said Pete. "She says it's all hype."

It took Janie several seconds to realize he was talking about the face on the milk carton. "What do you mean?" she said. She ate her peanut butter sandwich. Almost anything with peanut butter was excellent—peanut butter and marshmallow fluff; peanut butter and bananas—but a person needed milk to wash it down.

"All it is," said Pete firmly, "is divorce, where one parent gets mad and takes his own kid, but he doesn't tell the other parent where they're going. It's never actually a stranger stealing a kid, like on television."

"You mean they weren't really stolen?" said Sarah-Charlotte, vastly disappointed. She made several dramatic gestures. There was no room for dramatic gestures in the cafeteria, and people grabbed to save the whipped-cream towers on their Jell-O from getting splattered by Sarah-Charlotte's hands. "Nobody wants a ransom?" cried Sarah-Charlotte. "Nobody is being tortured?"

If I drink one carton of milk, Janie thought, is my allergy so serious I'll die? How boring the obituary would be: *Here lies Jane Johnson. I should leave a note: Put "Jayyne" on my stone.*

Janie shook her head.

Pete and Jason immediately complained that they had gotten red hair in their faces and would Janie please get a grip on her hair.

9

"What do you want me to do?" demanded Janie. "Wear a net around it?"

"Either that or build an addition to the cafeteria to house it," said Peter.

Everybody giggled.

Janie shook her hair more vigorously. The boys
ducked and threw potato chips at Janie, while
she reached for Sarah-Charlotte's milk and drank
it up.

Perfect meal. Peanut butter sandwich and a
glass of milk. Janie set the carton down and sighed
with pleasure.

The little girl on the back of the carton stared
back at her.

It wasn't much of a picture. After all, how good
could a picture be when it was printed on a milk
carton?

"You ready for that algebra test?" Jason asked
Adair.

"I was ready till I ate cafeteria food. Do you
think he'll let me out of the test if I have food
poisoning?"

The girl on the carton was an ordinary little
girl. Hair in tight pigtails, one against each thin
cheek. A dress with a narrow white collar. The
dress was white with tiny dark polka dots.

Something evil and thick settled on Janie,
blocking her throat, dimming her eyes. "Sarah-
Charlotte," she said. She could hear herself shouting Sarah-Charlotte's name, yet her lips were not
moving; she was making no sound at all.

She reached toward Sarah-Charlotte's sleeve,
but her hand didn't obey. It lay motionless on top

of the carton. It looked like somebody else's hand; she could not imagine herself wearing that shade of nail polish, or that silly ring.

"You drank my milk," accused Sarah-Charlotte.

"It's me on there," Janie whispered. Her head hurt. Was the milk allergy already setting in? Or was she going insane? Could you go insane this fast? Surely it took years to lose your mind.

She imagined people losing their minds the way you might lose a penny, or your car keys— accidentally dropping your mind in the cafeteria.

"On where?" said Peter.

"The girl on the back of the carton," whispered Janie. How flat her voice sounded. As if she had ironed it. "It's me."

She remembered that dress . . . how the collar itched . . . remembered the fabric; it was summer fabric; the wind blew through it . . . remembered how those braids swung like red silk against her cheeks.

"I know you're sick of school," said Sarah-Charlotte, "but claiming to be kidnapped is going a little too far, Janie."

Pete retrieved his flattened milk and tried to shape it back into a carton. He read between the folds. "You were stolen ten years ago from a shopping center in New Jersey, Janie. What are you doing here?"

"Yeah," said Adair, giggling. "Why aren't you off yelling for the police?"

"Oh, she's just trying to get out of reading her essay," said Jason.

"No, she's just trying to steal my milk," said Sarah-Charlotte.

The bell rang. The others hurled their garbage toward the huge plastic-lined trash cans by the door, and missed. Ducking under the plump arms of the lunch ladies, they raced back to class instead of picking it up.

Janie held Sarah-Charlotte's empty milk carton and stared at the photograph of the little girl.

I was kidnapped.

2

Janie learned that her body could function without her.

She lived entirely inside her mind, searching her memory like a little kid going through an encyclopedia, trying to find the right heading. *Jane Elizabeth Johnson, Kidnapping of.*

Her body, including her voice, her smile—even her knowledge (during sixth period she was actually able to answer questions in biology lab) —continued to work properly.

How interesting, Janie thought clinically. My body doesn't need me.

She had a sense of herself being brain dead: running on tubes and machines.

Inside, her mind spun. It was like having a color wheel for a brain. When it slowed down, things were separate, like primary colors: *I have a mother and father . . . I have a childhood . . . I was not kidnapped . . . kidnapping means bad people . . . I don't know any bad people . . . therefore I am making this up.*

But when her mind speeded up, the colors blended dizzily. *That is me on there. I, Janie Johnson; I was kidnapped.*

But it could not be.

The facts did not compute.

She tried to climb outside her mind and go where her body was: sitting neatly at a desk, neatly taking notes.

It was like crawling on glass. No matter how firmly she resolved not to think such stupid things, she thought them. She slithered backward into her mind.

Perhaps it's insanity, Janie thought. Perhaps I'm trapped in here with this horrible idea and I'll never get out. After a while people will notice and they'll lock up my body the way insanity has locked up my mind.

She discovered that school had ended.

Her body had gone to her locker. Taken the right books. Put on her jacket. Remembered the gym uniform that had to be washed. Said good-bye to friends and foe.

But slowly. Like someone trying to avoid the muddy parts in the grass. Her small body seemed to thicken, as if she had real iron in her blood and weighed several tons. The bus had left before she even arrived in the lobby. All the buses had left.

It was pouring rain.

The golden, gaudy-blue October had vanished and turned black and thundering. The sky at its richest: full of rage, ready to hit someone. It threw the rain against the pavement and ripped the leaves from the sugar maples.

A car headed for her. She watched the car, realizing that it was going to run her over: that somehow, although she was on the sidewalk, the car was aimed for her. Perhaps I should move, she thought. But nothing happened to her legs. They stayed there, holding her color-wheel brain in place, waiting to get run over.

"Get in quick," said Reeve, "before you get any wetter."

She had recognized neither him nor his Jeep. He had pulled the Jeep almost over her toes. The outside rearview mirror brushed the buttons on her jeans jacket. Janie got in slowly. This is fun, she thought. Now I'm paralyzed and blind, too.

Reeve said, "Let's ride down by the water. See if the tide is up over the road." Reeve loved floods. Two years ago there had been such a wonderful flood the families on the beach roads had to be rescued by the National Guard. Reeve had begged his parents to buy waterfront property so they could be in place for the next flood. They had uncooperatively said they liked it better a mile away on top of a hill. But Reeve kept an old battered canoe ready in the garage in case there should be another opportunity to paddle down the middle of the street. "A deluge like this," said Reeve happily, "a true Noah's Ark–type rain, you should have some decent flooding."

Janie nodded and turned the hot-air vents in her direction to dry her clothes. Her thick red hair sproinged up like a new permanent from the wetting it had taken.

"May I borrow your penknife?" she said.

"Sure." He detached the knife from his belt loop while she steered the Jeep. Then she couldn't get the blade to come up without breaking off a fingernail. Reeve stopped at a red light and opened the penknife for her.

Janie took the empty milk carton out of her book bag. She'd rinsed it out in the girls' room between fifth and sixth periods. She slit the carton open. Carefully she flattened it out. Then she opened her three-ring, blue-cloth English notebook, which had a clipboard on the inner front cover, and clipped the flat carton so that the photograph did not show. All Reeve could read was the logo FLOWER DAIRY, YOUR LOCAL MILK PRODUCER, SERVING ALL COMMUNITIES ON THE SHORELINE.

"That's an interesting hobby," observed Reeve. "You don't find too many milk carton collectors."

Janie thought about Pete's explanation. These so-called kidnappings are really just divorces, where one parent takes the child away and doesn't tell the other parent where they've gone.

Does that mean, she thought, that either my mother or my father is *not* my mother or my father? That somewhere out there is a *real* mother or a father who has wondered *for twelve years* where I am?

Reeve was staring out at the Atlantic Ocean, where the storm was hurling water and sand on the unprotected beaches. Reeve was handsomer than the rest of his family, yet there was a very strong resemblance among them. People could actually recognize Reeve by the smile that so much resembled his brother's, and the ruddy cheeks that were the trademark of his sisters. Now he was making terrible faces, flexing his forehead and lips and nose like Silly Putty because high tide had not managed to go over the road.

Reeve turned the Jeep into the Scenic Overlook, better known among teenagers as the Sexual Overlook because at night you could go there and watch couples in action. To the east stretched the ocean, and to the west, barely protected by thin spits of sand and mud, was the harbor where the wind jostled boats against the wharves. The boatyard was filled with marina employees taking boats out of the water for the winter storage. Even over the pounding of the waves and rain Janie could hear a strange smacking sort of applause. Not rigging hardware, nor waves against docks. "What's that noise?" she said. At least I'm not deaf, she thought.

"Flags," said Reeve. American flags, everywhere: on the docks, at the fuel pumps, on the boats. Each clapped in the fierce wind like a cloth maniac. "I'm sort of like a flag," said Reeve.

"Red, white, and blue?"

"No. A big banner flapping in the wind. YOU'RE DUMB, says the flag. My sisters, my brother, my parents: they don't say it out loud, but they kind of line up my college application forms next to my grades and my SATs and the old flag waves, YOU'RE DUMB."

"You're not dumb," said Janie, although he

was. She adored Reeve, but brains would round him out a bit.

"My parents haven't taken me to see any college campuses," said Reeve. "Nor arranged any interviews. Nothing. For Megan and Lizzie and Todd we spent a year apiece visiting and pondering and drawing up lists and pros and cons. With me, they've already given up. They don't yell at me anymore. You know what my mother said to your mother?"

"No," said Janie, although she did; her mother had repeated it, of course. Or is she my mother? thought Janie. Is she Daddy's second wife? Did they steal me from my real mother? Or is it Daddy who is somebody else? Maybe they're not even married. Maybe they just—

"Your mother said to my mother, 'At least you can be proud of Megan, Lizzie, and Todd,' and then my mother said, 'That's true, three out of four isn't bad.' "

Nobody else in my family has red hair, thought Janie. I don't laugh like Mother and Daddy. My fingernails aren't shaped like theirs. "That's terrible," she said to Reeve. "They're being rotten, writing you off like that."

"I'll be lucky to get into the community college," said Reeve. He fiddled with the radio dials and the heater knobs, flicked the emergency blinkers on and off, and pawed through the cassettes he had in the Jeep.

"At least you have a Jeep to commute in," said Janie, but this was not a comfort to Reeve, who wanted to be brilliant, outstanding, impressive, and memorable, like his brother and sisters.

18

She opened her notebook. She tilted it and peered at the back of the milk carton. It was still her on there.

She had not allowed herself to read the name under the photograph. Now she read it.

Jennie Spring.

Her brain stopped being a color wheel and became an echo chamber—*Jennie Spring Jennie Spring Jennie Spring Jennie*—

"What have you got in there?" teased Reeve. He reached for the notebook to see what forbidden article was stashed in it. Janie jerked it back. "No, Reeve, don't," she said urgently, and he was startled, pulling his hand back as if maybe it were a scorpion inside the English notebook.

Reeve left the Scenic Overlook so fast they hydroplaned over the puddles. Then he gnashed the gears, roaring forward along the narrow, wet beach road, skidding purposely. He took each gear up to its highest RPMs so the motor screamed. He jerked left into the traffic on Route 1. Like a warrior he battled the cars and the rain, pedal to the metal, taking off from each stop sign like a chariot racer.

Janie touched her seat belt and said nothing. She would feel that way, too, if she were Reeve. While he was passing in a no-passing zone, Janie turned the milk-carton cover over again.

The little girl's name and birthdate, the 800 number to call if you recognized her, the place from which she vanished in New Jersey. None of it meant a thing to Janie.

I've always felt a year younger than Sarah-Charlotte and Adair, thought Janie. And if that's my birthday, I *am* a year younger. I'm not old enough to get my driver's license after all.

But it was too ridiculous. She had a family. A perfectly normal family. They loved her. She loved them.

"I don't feel like going home yet, do you?" said Reeve. He spoke in the voice people use when you have to agree or walk home. Besides, she did agree. She had hardly ever agreed with anything more.

"Let's get ice cream," said Reeve. He jerked the wheel hard, turned across traffic with far too little time, and just barely missed getting a pickup truck through the side of his Jeep. The trucker rightly leaned on his horn. Janie gave him an apologetic smile and the town wave.

The trucker grinned at Janie. She shook her red hair at him and the guy grinned even wider.

Perhaps I'm fascinating after all, she thought. That trucker forgave Reeve because I tossed my hair. He'd believe me if I said my name was Jayyne Jonstone.

"I don't have any money," she told Reeve. "And I can't have ice cream." But what if my name is Jennie Spring? she thought.

"I'll pay. Anyway, I saw you drinking milk for lunch. You've already broken the rules."

He saw me drinking Sarah-Charlotte's milk, she thought. Which I drank long after he waved. So he looked back. Checked me out a second time.

They went to a booth, passing two groups of teenagers she knew by sight but not by name. All eyes landed on Reeve with Janie and drew conclusions. Janie was not sure she liked this. It was not a date; poor Reeve was just having to admit he was dumb; Janie was his trusty, rusty, next-door neighbor.

Reeve ordered two hot-fudge sundaes on one scoop each of vanilla and chocolate mint. For years when they were little kids going shopping with their mothers, this had been Janie's order. She had changed preferences since the last time she had had ice cream with Reeve; up till the lactose intolerance discovery, she'd ordered vanilla with butterscotch topping. She said nothing. She was quite touched that Reeve remembered.

Reeve talked about first-quarter grades, which were coming up in only a few weeks. He talked about the horror of failing his senior year; of having to go to a lousy college when Megan, Lizzie, and Todd went to such winners; the horror of all school at all times.

The waitress brought the sundaes much more quickly than usual and Janie thanked her. She turned to look at her sundae.

The world shifted.

Friendly Ice Cream seemed to spin around her, all its flavors, all its booths, tilting and screaming.

She was sitting with somebody else.

Sitting on a high stool—a stool that swiveled— she was turning herself slowly and carefully by holding on to the counter—her feet did not touch the foot rest—she was little—she was admiring her white cotton socks as she turned because they had a little strip of lace—

21

A woman was next to her—not swiveling— long, straight hair cascading down the woman's back, so pretty Janie had to touch it. The woman kept her hand in the air behind Janie's back so she wouldn't tip off the spinning stool.

Janie was having a sundae—whipped cream on it—eating the cherry off her sundae first and then one off the woman's sundae.

They were laughing.

Janie was little—the woman hugged her— swung her around as the stool had swung—

—there was a hot wind—they were outside now; in a huge parking lot; maybe the biggest parking lot in the world—her dress, white with tiny dark dots, blew in the air—

"Janie?" said Reeve. "Are you all right?"

Janie's mouth was dry, her hands icy. She was shivering all over. She could feel the tiny table shaking from her shivers. Reeve was frightened.

"Are you getting the flu?" he said. He put his hand out as if to stop her from crossing some terrible road. "You're not really *seriously* allergic to milk, are you? I mean, is your throat going to close up or your heart stop?" She was aware that he was calling her. Raising his voice. That people were looking. "Janie? Janie, are you okay?" His hand took hers and to her frozen fingers his hand felt like a furnace, as if he were going to scorch her.

"I'm fine," she said. "Dizzy."

She had always had control over her daydreams; like the daydreams of Denim and Lace in which she designed every detail to suit herself. She had never had a daydream that dreamed itself, like nightmares. That crawled out of her brain like a creature of the dark.

A daymare.

Janie shuddered. "I'd better not eat the sundae," she said. Already the daymare was fading, leaving her flesh like jelly, but no pictures to remember it by. Woman, she thought dimly, stool, dress, hot wind.

It must be, thought Janie, that my life is boring. Deep down I must be as angry over the boredom as Reeve is over being dumb. He drives like a maniac to feel better and I fall into maniac daydreams. My parents are my parents. Nobody kidnapped me. I don't really remember the dress.

Reeve called to the waitress. "Could we have these to go?" He pointed at Janie. "She doesn't feel well."

"They'll be messy," said the waitress doubtfully. "The top will be on the bottom."

Tell me about it, thought Janie.

CHAPTER
3

There were no cars in the driveway. Her father couldn't be coaching soccer in this weather so he would be pulling in any moment now. Her mother must be at the hospital—what day was this?—she volunteered two days a week.

The Johnsons' driveway was separated from Reeve's by a thin row of shrubs over which Megan, Lizzie, Todd, and now Reeve continually backed. Only hours ago Janie had thought joyously of the day when she, too, learning reverse, would flatten a few bushes.

"You sure you'll be all right?" said Reeve. "I could ask Mom to go over and sit with you."

"Please," said Janie, meaning no, and they both laughed. When Reeve's mother took care of a person, she took serious care—bed rest, chicken soup, and pillow fluffing. On school-nurse forms, Janie had always put Reeve's mother to phone in an emergency, and Reeve had always put Janie's mother. Reeve's mother always sat with Janie, rubbing her back, reading chapters from long books. Janie had to be in the mood for all that loving kindness. More often, when she was sick, she just wanted to be alone, in the silence and the nest of her bed.

How can I be kidnapped? thought Janie. I don't even have neighbors who understand evil, let alone parents.

She got out of the Jeep and dashed through the rain, putting her key in the side door. This opened onto a landing on the stairs between the cellar and the kitchen. Down in the cellar next to the gleaming-white washer and dryer, her folded jeans were stacked. Up in the kitchen lay a pile of mail, an overflowing brown paper bag marked for the Salvation Army, and the breakfast dishes.

She scraped the dishes and loaded the dishwasher. It wasn't full enough to run. There was a note on the refrigerator in her mother's pretty script: *Darling—don't forget class tonight, home by supper, love Mommy.*

Janie hadn't called her mother Mommy in years, though she still called her father Daddy. Class? she thought, trying to make sense of that reminder.

She walked through the house, touching. Same furniture: her mother liked deep, intense colors: the sofa and chairs were a blue so dark and rich they invited you like a deep sea to dive in. In the dining room two walls were glass and one was bright red; the only decoration was an enormous framed color photograph of Janie, age twelve, bridesmaid for a wedding. She was giggling in the picture, half bent over, trying to hold her tiara of

25

flowers as it slid off her red hair. Janie disliked the portrait: she hadn't gotten her braces yet and the uneven teeth seemed to take over the entire picture. But her parents loved it. "How you adored that long dress!" they would say, smiling into the photograph's eyes, as if it were as alive. "How proud you were, being in the wedding party, dancing with the groom, staying up till dawn."

Janie climbed the stairs to her room, passing by the ascending wall of photographs. Her parents disliked albums; they immortalized Janie on the stairs. Janie at the beach, on skis, in a Scout uniform, in her first dancing dress. Janie on their trip to the Grand Canyon. Janie in gymnastics, Janie at the Middle School Awards Ceremony. Janie on the runway for the fashion show the hospital sponsored as a benefit.

I'm sick, she thought. Deranged. Imagine imagining they kidnapped me! I mean, talk about proof of loving family. From the folded laundry to the refrigerator note—

She remembered what the class was.

Her mother had decided that she and Janie needed An Activity to Share. She'd picked, of all things, cake decorating. In spite of their past record at arts and crafts—the failed needlepoint pillows, the abandoned quilt tops, the unfinished knitting—her mother was convinced that she and Janie could be like the rest of the world and do something creative with their hands.

The only thing Janie liked to do with her hands was put nail polish on them and dial phone numbers.

. . . phone numbers . . .

On the milk carton was a toll-free, 800 number to dial. *If you have seen this child . . .*

Janie froze three steps from the top. Turning her head slowly, like a patient becoming paralyzed, neck stiffening forever, she forced her eyes to search among the photographs.

There were no baby pictures.

She had asked why before. Because they never got around to buying a camera till Janie was five, said her parents.

But you didn't need your own camera for baby photographs. Every single store that sold baby clothes—from Sears to Bloomingdale's, from High-Fashion Tot to Toys R Us—had photographers; and special portrait prices.

Jennie Spring. Taken from a shopping center in New Jersey at age three.

But I should remember, thought Janie. Three years old is time to have memories. It's not as if Jennie Spring was three months old.

She entered her room. It was the largest bedroom in the house. Since her parents each had a small study, they had taken the little bedroom and given her the spacious master bedroom. Janie had a habit of leaping into hobbies with tremendous enthusiasm for a few months and then abandoning them forever. The walls and shelves were testimony to lost interests. There was the gymnastics display, when she had fallen in love with tumbling. There were the horseback-riding ribbons, from fourth grade when she practically lived at the stable. There was the music, when she had intended to be the world's foremost flutist. The last piece she had ever practiced still lay open on the pretty little music stand her parents had bought her for Christmas that year.

Janie did not share her mother's adoration of fierce, intense blues and reds. When she turned fourteen, they had redecorated the room by Janie's colors: ivory, pale pale rose, and faded lavender. The bedspread Janie had chosen was lace panels: all different shades and textures of white. It was too fragile to sit on. She folded the lace into a tube at the bottom of her bed and lay down on the plain, dark-rose wool blanket beneath it. She was as rigid as a board. The mattress sank down while Janie's spine remained stiff. She ordered her muscles to relax, forcing first her shoulders to go limp, then her neck, and her jaw.

At last she had sagged into the contours of the mattress. Now she tried to look inside her brain, to dip through her memory as if it were a card catalog at the library.

Nothing.

And yet—memory felt oddly bright—not dark— not scary or mysterious—light . . . easy . . . good.

There's somebody else down there, thought Janie.

She shuddered violently, picturing another tiny little girl living at the bottom of her body, begging to get out.

Janie wet her lips.

The silence of the house was suddenly unbearable. She leaped from the bed, pounded down the stairs, flung open the side door, and ran over to the Shieldses' house.

They were too close friends with the Shieldses to bother much with knocking. She opened the door, yelled, "Hello," and went on in. Mrs. Shields was watching *Lassie*.

"There's probably something wrong with me," remarked Reeve's mother, "but I adore all these old black-and-white reruns. They're so safe."

Safe, thought Janie.

"Is not safe," said Reeve, coming into the room. He had his physics lab book with him. The sight of Reeve with an academic text in his hand startled Janie. "Timmy and Lassie are always saving somebody from runaway trains or bottomless swamps or forest fires."

"Ah, but the kitchen!" said Mrs. Shields. "Nothing ever goes wrong in the kitchen. Have a chocolate chip cookie, dear," she said to Janie.

"Don't," advised Reeve. "She put icky things like oatmeal and bran into the cookies. Timmy," he told his mother, referring to Lassie's owner, "would never have had to gag down oatmeal and bran in *his* cookies."

Nevertheless Reeve took several of the largest cookies and flung himself into a chair. He was one of those boys who don't simply sit: they collapse, snapping the legs off chairs and breaking the backs of couches. Janie and his mother waited for Reeve to fall on through to the floor, but the chair held him once more.

"Mrs. Shields?" said Janie. "How long have you lived here?"

"Darling, I am that rara avis. A native. I was born here."

"I mean, in this house."

"Twenty-eight years. Bought it when we were married."

"Do you remember when we moved here?"

"I certainly do. You were the most adorable five-year-old who ever drew breath on Romney Road. And your mother was the strictest parent. I shaped up once she moved in, let me tell you." Mrs. Shields smiled, a private smile of memories kept within, to warm herself by.

"Why was she so strict?" said Janie. She had bitten off some cookie and now was unable to chew it. Little bits of dough and bran lay on her tongue and threatened to choke her.

"Because you were so bad," said Reeve immediately.

He and his mother laughed. "No, Janie was always sweet, good, obedient, and courteous," said Mrs. Shields. "I used to yearn for a Janie among my four wild animals."

Why was I such a goody-goody? thought Janie. Was I afraid? If they stole me, I should have been afraid of *them*, not the rest of the world. "Seriously," said Janie.

Mrs. Shields watched *Lassie*. Timmy's mother was wearing her apron. In old television they always had on aprons.

Janie fell into another nightmare by daylight. Her mind plummeted down into the nightmare the way Reeve's muscular body had fallen onto the upholstery.

Apron.

It was white; heavy; almost as heavy as canvas; it had a bib; her mother kept little hard candies in one pocket and Janie could stretch up and reach her baby hand into the pocket to take out one candy. With a cellophane wrapper that crinkled.

But my mother doesn't wear aprons, thought Janie.

"Life isn't like that now," said Mrs. Shields sadly. "Too many dreadful possibilities out there. And hardly any Lassies to save you. Mothers have nightmares about their babies, Janie—from drowning in a neighbor's swimming pool to snapping the spine playing football. I think all mothers fear that one dreadful accident—when the child dashes out in front of a truck. When some maniac snatches the child during the one second the mother isn't looking. Your mother has always felt that way, Janie. She's always been afraid."

"For what reason?" said Janie. She forced herself to swallow the dead cookie in her mouth. Reeve, becoming a host, which was almost as unthinkable as Reeve becoming a scholar, handed her a Coke.

"What mother ever needed a reason?" said Mrs. Shields. "I suppose because you were the only child. I had three earlier ones to take out my unreasonable fears on. Old Reeve here, I didn't worry about him much because I'd used up so much worry on the others."

She and Reeve began a teasing verbal battle about how much worry he had caused her in his seventeen years, and was likely to cause in the next seventeen.

Janie stayed till the end of *Lassie*. The final scene was in the kitchen. Timmy of course had a glass of milk. Nobody in old television gave their kids soda. It ended happily ever after, with hugs all around and a barking collie.

"Oh, my goodness, I'm late!" cried her mother, throwing open the front door. Her mother never came in the side door. She liked to look around the front hall, with its graceful mirrors and slender, elegant furniture, and into the beautiful living room she had designed. "Janie, by any wonderful chance did you start supper? We have our cake decorating class tonight. We've got to leave in thirty minutes. What's in the freezer? Anything we can microwave? Did you do your homework? How was school?"

She gave Janie a big hug and a little row of kisses down her cheek toward her throat. "Daddy home yet?"

"No." Janie stared at her mother. She tried to imagine her mother as a kidnapper, rushing into shopping malls and jerking little girls off soda fountain stools. But her mother was elegant, formal. She could imagine her mother raising funds for a scholarship for this little girl—but actually snatching her? Mother liked to conduct her meetings properly, with much consulting of formal Rules of Order.

"Oh, dear, I hate it when we leave in the evening without seeing him. I hate not having dinner together. I read the other day that most families in America now have separate meals—each one just grabs a bite on the run, a pizza here, a frozen Weight Watchers casserole there. I think that's so sad, families no longer sitting down together every evening. And here we are, just like all the rest. I hate being just like all the rest."

Well, you're not, thought Janie. You're a kidnapper.

Her mother was beautifully dressed. She hung up her crimson wool coat and slipped off her high, slim heels. Her feet were very long and very narrow and finding shoes was a real trial. Janie's feet were short and wide.

There's nothing in me that's like her, thought Janie. Is it because I have none of her genes? Because she is not my mother?

She forced herself to think of Adair O'Dell, who was so sleek. Adair's mother was a fat, messy woman whose offspring you would expect to be total rug rats. So lots of times kids didn't resemble their parents. It meant nothing.

Her father charged in the side door, full of energy from soccer. "What a team!" he said. He launched his first bear hug at his wife, and Janie would normally have run up for hers, but she found herself edging out of reach. "What a season. I love my kids. They try so hard! We practiced in the school gym because of the rain. Can't stand that stupid principal they have down there. Good janitor, though. Big help. I can't wait for the next game. We have so much potential this year! Why are we having microwave pizza? Where are you guys going? Don't I even get to talk to my girl?" He pretended to kick soccer balls around Janie's ankles.

"Daddy, stop it," she said.

"How can I embarrass you when there's nobody around to see?" he countered. "Tell you what. I promise to do this in front of all your friends one day, just for comparison's sake."

"Thanks," said Janie.

"Cake decorating," explained her mother.

"Do you think it's the right sort of class for somebody as weight obsessed as you are?" said her father.

"I won't eat any of it," said her mother virtuously.

"Sure," said her father. "Listen, you two scarf down those awful frozen jobs. I'll make myself a real dinner after my shower. Love ya. Have fun. Bring me some cake. I want the most frosting." He charged up the stairs.

They talk more than I do, too, thought Janie. They spout conversation continually, both of them. I have more listening in me than talking.

The class was at the Y. The familiar hot-chlorine-and-sweat smell of the pool met their noses.

"Remember your swim team?" said her mother. "I was so glad you lost interest in swimming. There I'd sit, with all the other mothers, waiting for hours till your heat came up, and then I couldn't even tell which one you were and it was over in three minutes anyhow. Ugh. At least when you took up riding, it was more fun. Why don't you go back to riding?"

"I would have if I'd known the alternative was cake decorating," said Janie. "Mom, I'm dreading this. We've bombed out on watercolor, decoupage . . ."

"Well, you couldn't eat any of those. The taste tests will make all the difference." They took the stairs to the kitchen. The Y ran a soup kitchen by day (where her mother had not yet volunteered but surely would before long), but in the evenings the kitchen was available to cooking classes. Japanese, Chinese, Vietnamese, and French cooking each had a night. Cake decorating seemed backward and untrendy next to those cuisines.

"Think of all the calories. This is a dangerous hobby, Mom. Besides, you told Daddy you weren't going to eat any."

"I lied."

Janie and her mother burst into giggles.

There were nine in the class. Janie was the only one under forty and the only one not watching her pounds. "I'm going to like this," whispered her mother. "Next to you, I'm the skinniest person here."

They learned on cardboard, not cakes. They piped icing out of tubes, cloth bags, and paper cones. They used star tips and tube tips for flowers and ribbons. Janie could not keep the pressure on her tube even, so that for every attractive flower, she had a pitiful plop of icing instead. "Yours looks like a very faded bouquet," remarked her mother.

The instructor demonstrated flowers yet again. As Janie leaned forward to see the technique, she fell hideously into another daymare.

The conscious part of her thought: Am I falling into the cake? Will I be a pitiful fool in front of these women, my face covered with icing?

The daymare was white: white flowers, white whipped cream, white ice cream. *The pretty woman, the whirling stool at the counter. And white shoes: tiny, shiny white shoes.*

We were shoe shopping, thought Janie. But who is "we"? Who am I?

"Now you try," said the instructor, putting the tube in her hand. Janie struggled to make a flower, but there was no white icing in the tube. There was a thin line of blue gel instead. She stared at the demonstration cake and saw that while she had been lost in a dreadful white dream, they had changed from flowers to writing.

Her hand shook. She tried to write HAPPY BIRTH-DAY.

What was the birth date on the carton? she thought. When was Jennie Spring's birthday? Is it mine?

CHAPTER
4

She slept soundly.

If she dreamed, she did not remember when she awoke.

How strange, thought Janie. You'd think if anything would give me nightmares, it would be this.

She got out of bed. Janie loved nightwear. Sometimes she was in a pajama mood and she had flannel pajamas, silk shortie pajamas, and sweet cotton-and-lace pajamas. Sometimes she preferred nightgowns and she had everything from bridal-trousseau-type gowns to teddies. But recently she had gotten into sweatshirt stuff: this new gown was a soft pearl gray, like a sweatshirt to the floor.

She peeled the gown up and over her head and stared at herself, naked in the mirror. She liked her body.

Morning sun streamed in the window. It caught on the prisms Janie had been given for some elementary-school science project and never taken

37

down from their plastic strings. Miniature rainbows danced across the walls. She held out her hand and "caught" one in her palm.

On the desk was a spray of reference books given her over various Christmases and rarely touched. The dictionary was a huge dark-blue Webster's. She looked up nightmare. From Middle English *niht*—"night"—and Anglo-Saxon *mare*—"demon." Then she looked up "daydream." "A pleasant, dreamy thought."

Below it, there actually was a word "daymare." Defined as a nightmare taking place in the day.

Demon, thought Janie. That's what it was. Some demon—some goblin or troll—forcing a daymare on me.

In school the boys were particularly sophomoric.

Janie adored mischief, if she could watch rather than participate. She was perfectly willing to cheer the boys on as long as she ran no risk of getting punished along with them.

Pete had a huge roll of masking tape left over from an art project.

All the kids were attracted by the tape. Everybody wanted to rip off a piece and tape things together. "We could tape Sarah-Charlotte's mouth shut," said Jason, laughing, ready to do it.

"Tape the trash-barrel lids closed so nobody can throw anything away," Adair suggested.

"Or tape Ellen Winter's braids to her back!" Nobody liked Ellen Winter. Nobody ever had, nobody ever would. The poor thing would have nobody to untape her.

"No, let's tape Janie's hair down!" cried Jason.

"At last I'll have breathing space during lunch. We'll just wind the whole roll around her forehead until her hair is finally under control."

Janie shrieked with mixed horror and delight, protecting her head with her arms. She considered whether to yank her sweater up over her hair and run screaming down the halls. Sarah-Charlotte shuddered, imagining this fate. "You'd never get it off! When we pulled the tape away, we'd scalp her! You sadist. Somebody lock this boy up. He's sick and twisted."

"I like that in a person," said Adair.

"I know," said Pete. "Let's tape all the desks together."

"Let's what?"

"Let's go into the ninth-grade wing. They're all at lunch. We'll turn every desk inward and tape them together. When they get back from lunch, they won't be able to get their chairs under the desks."

"Ooooh, that's a great idea," said Sarah-Charlotte. "What a gift from us to them. Think how they'll waste a whole period trying to untape desks."

There was silence while each debated whether the pleasure would be worth the pain, if they got caught, or whether they'd rather just sit there and have lunch, or if they'd be wimps if they didn't follow through on it now.

Adair, who was going for her driver's test the following Monday, and who carried her driver's ed book with her everywhere, was not interested. "Don't let's do that," she begged. "Somebody test me on stopping distance instead."

Janie flipped the book open and read aloud the

questions on stopping distances. Adair got them all right. She had the entire book memorized.

"I'm so afraid I'll forget something when I go for my test," said Adair. "What if they won't give me my license just because I didn't remember to bring my birth certificate?"

"Then we'd know what a dumbbell you are," said Jason. "If you're that dumb, you don't deserve your brownie, so give me your dessert."

Janie's body turned to ice.

I have no more control over my temperature than I do over the daymares, thought Janie. She said, "You have to have a birth certificate to get a driver's license, Adair?" Now her interior betrayed her: all the organs in her chest and abdomen shuddered and rippled.

I don't want to know, thought Janie. Because . . . because why? Does something deep inside me know already? But why now? Why haven't I known all along? How could you forget something like your real family and the moment you were taken from them? I know I'm making it up; it's a demon, the dictionary says so.

So why am I turning cold with fear?

"Three forms of identification," said Adair. "I'm bringing my birth certificate, which you have to have, my Social Security card, and my passport."

Jason laughed suddenly. "I remember the first time I saw my birth certificate," he said, "with its little raised seal and the gold lettering at the top, and it was so official and all: the real me: and it had the *wrong* birth date. I practically passed out. I thought—*I'm somebody else, I'm adopted, they switched babies at the hospital.* I sweated so much the paper got soggy."

Janie's mouth was so dry she could not ask questions.

"It turns out," Jason explained, his voice rich with relief, "that there are two dates: the day you were born and the day they register you on the records, which in my case was several days later. My eyes landed on the wrong date."

Janie seemed to melt, like ice cream in the sun.

She had no energy left, hardly even a mind. She pictured road surfaces in winter, ripped into potholes and heaves by the changing temperatures, ice one day, sunny thaw the next. Would the changing temperatures of her imagination rip through her, too? She had never seen an insane person. They don't mean to go insane, thought Janie. It happens to their surface, like freeze and thaw.

She had a sense that she must hold on to her sanity, the way in a crowd in the city you held on to your purse. That it would take both hands to stay sane.

Reeve did not give her a ride home.

She took the bus.

It stopped at the corner; she had a block to walk.

Theirs was an architecturally mixed neighborhood. Originally a street of substantial older houses with front porches, big attics, and trees that dumped a million leaves every autumn, each side lot had been built upon. Modern ranches and cute little Cape Cods lay between each brown-shingled old place. Her own house was an old one dramatically modernized with sheets of glass where once there had been dark, hidden rooms.

Janie walked through mountains of leaves in the gutter, waiting for the town crew to come with the frightening leaf-vacuum that sucked and then minced the scarlet and gold leaves. She had never been able to watch it.

She went in the side door. "Mom?" she yelled.

"In here, dear." Her mother was at her desk. Lists, folders, notations. All the stuff for her various causes and crusades. "How was school, darling?"

"Oh, you know. School."

"I had a great day," said her mother happily. "My Laotian boy. He's really made a quantum leap. He's not going to need me much longer." Her mother tutored English as a second language. The Laotian boy had one interest, and one only: sports. He wanted his terms straight so he wouldn't refer to "baskets" or "goals" for a baseball game.

"Mom?" said Janie, keeping her voice light. "I'm going to need my birth certificate for getting my driver's license. Can I see it now?"

Her mother's pencil stopped moving on the form she was filling out.

It seemed to Janie that her mother's knuckles tightened and whitened. Her mother said, "Darling, you won't be eligible for months."

"I know, but Adair's been talking about it and I got interested."

"It's in the safe deposit box at the bank," said her mother.

"Oh. Well, then, let's go open it."

"I'm very busy, darling."

"Let's go tomorrow then."

"Tomorrow's Saturday," said her mother quickly. "The bank's not open."

Janie felt like an executioner, escorting her own mother to the guillotine. "Monday then," said Janie.

Her mother said, "Jane Elizabeth Johnson, you do not give your mother orders, do you hear me? You may ask courteously, but you may not command."

"Why don't you want me to see my birth certificate?" said Janie.

Her mother turned a page in her notebook and stared at the blank paper. "Don't be ridiculous, Janie. Now let's have a snack. What do you feel like? I did a huge grocery shopping. New microwave and frozen stuff we haven't tried yet. And fruit juice popsicles for you instead of ice cream."

She doesn't want me to see my birth certificate, thought Janie. Because there isn't one? Because the dates are wrong? Or because she isn't in the mood to bother with the bank?

In the kitchen Janie looked in the breadbox and passed on doughnuts, fresh onion bagels, and raspberry coffee cake. She checked the shelves but did not feel like opening Double Stuf Oreos or Mallomars. She was not in the mood for the strawberry-vanilla yogurt or leftover pizza in the refrigerator. "I knew all along my snack would be in the freezer," she remarked.

But her mother had not come in with her.

Janie turned slowly, looking around the empty room.

Always, after school, if her mother was home, the two of them shared snacks, discussed their day, opened the mail together.

Her mother not only remained in her study; she had even shut the door.

Janie jerked open the freezer. Cold air bathed her cheeks. There was a quart of Wildberry Ripple Ice Cream, Flavor of the Month, for her father.

From the shelf she took her favorite bowl, a Peter Rabbit bowl she had had—since when? thought Janie. All my life? Or since I was—

She wrenched her mind away from it.

From the utensil drawer she took the ice cream scoop.

It was old, with a wooden handle now split from many runs through the dishwasher. The scoop itself was pitted with age.

Like a painting from the bottom up, another kitchen emerged in her brain. She saw the floor first—toys on it—yellow linoleum. She saw the legs of chairs next, and the legs of grown-ups. Then a tabletop—it was at eye level—she was the height of the table.

Janie panted like a child having an asthma attack.

She could barely keep her balance.

The painting grew, gathering color and detail.

. . . not a large room . . . messy . . . two screaming babies, each in a high chair . . . the apron: that white canvas apron with the pocket of candy . . . a bag of Wonder Bread; she could

44

remember the wrapper . . . her voice asking for
milk . . . but nobody heard her over the scream-
ing of the babies, so Janie got it herself, spilling
a puddle. She could remember mopping it up
with a paper towel, proud of herself for making
the mess and for unmaking it. . . . She remem-
bered being scooped up, hugged . . . laughter
. . . noise . . . mess . . . commotion . . .

The kitchen in which she really stood was large, smooth, and empty. The counters and shelves pounded in her head, like cartoon things taking on life and rhythm.

Abandoning the quart of Wildberry Ripple, Janie ran outside.

Reeve was raking leaves in his yard. "Hi," he said, "come to help? I've got an extra rake. It's time you earned your keep, woman." He grinned. His face was rather long and narrow, and the grin was a surprise, because it took up so much space—you were socked with joy when Reeve smiled at you. A French-looking beret tilted on his hair. He was thigh-deep in leaves. "I've got to mow the lawn again," he explained. "That grass went and grew some more. I don't know how, under a foot of leaves. Here. Rake, Janie. I need you."

She took the rake. Energy spilled out of her like oil from a smashed tanker. Leaves were flung into the air. She made immense, immediate progress.

Reeve stared at her.

She raked on and on, until the leaves were a mountain in front of her and the lawn a green swarm behind her.

Without catching himself, Reeve fell backward into the leaf pile and sank toward the ground, brown leaves sliding over his face and chest. "Janie, you have a problem? Come tell Uncle Reeve." He sprawled comfortably. The leaves crackled with every breath he took.

She sat next to him, cross-legged, looking down into his face. They were in a nest, hidden from the adult world. There was nothing like a pile of leaves to make you feel little again. "Reeve, do you think 800 numbers can trace a call? I mean, if you called an 800 number and didn't say anything, could they find out what phone you called from?"

"I take it you're not going to call *Time* magazine for a subscription," said Reeve, laughing. "Who are you calling? The Secret Service to report an assassination attempt?"

How did he get so close? she thought. Does he know something, too? Deep down, without admitting it, does he remember? He would have been seven, I would have been five. "I thought I'd call the Milk Council to find out about new research on milk allergies," she said.

Reeve shouted with laughter. "Oh, boy, they'll really want to trace that call, Jane Elizabeth. They'll figure they've got an escaped, drug-running Central American dictator on the phone for sure when you ask about milk allergies." He laughed and laughed, put both hands around her, and pulled her down into the leaves with him.

5

The kiss was long.

And serious.

Serious like my hair, thought Janie. She stared amazed at Reeve's cheek, which was pressed against hers, and with amazement brought her lips together to kiss him again—to start the second kiss, and to choose when to end it. She could feel his heart racing and then felt her own pick up speed and run with his.

Very slowly her hands crept around his face, finding the back of his neck where his hair lay thick over the pulse. His hand, rough-surfaced, gently touched her face. Moved her hair away. With the pad of his thumb he traced her profile.

"Reeve!" shouted his mother from the house. "Reeve, where are you? Phone call! It's Michael."

They fell apart, each lying back on crinkly leaves, staring at the sky. Reeve said, "Uh—Michael probably wants to know if—um—well—I better talk to him."

"Okay," said Janie.

She stood up first and began dusting the leaves off herself. She could feel leaf bits in her hair and down the back of her sweater. Reeve's eyes fixed on her hair and he moved as if to brush the leaves away for her, but then he looked down at his feet instead, mumbling, "See you," and ran into the house.

Janie's heart and lungs were working as if they were trying to power a city's electricity. She picked up the rake again. Their two bodies had left prints on the leaf pile, like angels in the snow. She raked the pile back together, until the prints were hidden, and the evidence gone.

Reeve did not come back from his phone call.

The sun went behind clouds and she was cold.

She went inside, remembering the ice cream on the counter and wondering if it had melted everywhere. But her mother had put it away. "That showed such discipline, Janie," her mother complimented her. "To get exercise instead of indulging in forbidden foods!" An I've-got-a-secret smile spread on her mother's face. "Look," she said. "I've been practicing. What do you think of it?"

From the refrigerator she took a large rectangular pan covered with aluminum foil, which Janie had thought was lasagne. Peeling back the foil, her mother showed off a sheet cake. The cake was iced in white, with purple piping on the sides—and a cute little purple football arching over purple goalposts in the center. "Tomorrow we're all driving up to the university for the football game," said her mother. "I'm doing dessert.

Usually I go to the bakery and order lots of chocolate surprises, but this time I thought I'd do a cake. What do you think of it?"

"It's so cute!" cried Janie. "Look, you even have the little team over here, painted in gel. And here's a cheerleader. Mom, I love her pom-poms. How did you do it?"

Each year they went for a tailgate picnic along with Reeve's family and Sarah-Charlotte's. The football game! she thought. I'll be with Reeve tomorrow. All day. Her heart raced.

"I was in a Grandma Moses mood," explained her mother. "I decided to do a primitive painting in purple tube art on a cake."

They giggled. For the first time in her life, Janie regretted that Sarah-Charlotte would be along, with her eagle eyes and endless chatter.

"I just hope the cake is edible," said her mother. "I haven't baked a cake in a hundred years. I used Duncan Hines mix, though, so I'm probably safe."

"There's no way to taste-test," agreed Janie. "Unless we cut off the goalposts and eat them tonight."

"Bite your tongue. This took me the entire day, Janie. My goodness, what's in your hair?"

"Leaves," said Janie. "I went out to help Reeve rake and he got silly and we fell over in the leaf pile like a pair of third graders."

With Janie sitting on a kitchen chair and her mother standing behind her, she brushed and brushed till the red hair was full of static and the floor covered with tiny brown bits of leaf.

Janie thought of Reeve. Those leaves on the

floor might be the only souvenir of her only kisses. When he ran away to take Michael's phone call, had he also been running away from the kiss he had given Janie? "I think I'll do my weekend homework tonight," said Janie, "since the football game will take all day Saturday." She took back her hairbrush and went upstairs to be alone with the memory of Reeve, and his lips, and his rough-soft hand.

Usually she passed her so-called homework hours on the phone with Sarah-Charlotte or Adair. There were also Gretchen, Doria, and Michelle to call if Sarah-Charlotte's and Adair's phones were busy.

Janie was almost overcome with the desire to talk about Reeve. *He kissed me, he pulled me down in the leaves, like somebody in a romance novel where the man is so frantic with passion he pulls her off the horse, or out of the carriage, and onto the bed. You should have been there! It was incredible.*

However, Sarah-Charlotte, who liked things nailed down on all four sides, would demand, "So did he ask you out? Are you dating? What kind of commitment did you get from him?"

So she wouldn't call Sarah-Charlotte. And maybe not Adair either, because Adair would hate the part about getting leaves in her hair. Adair was against anything messy.

Janie sighed and opened her book bag, dumping the contents on her bed. She never studied at her desk. She used the desktop for her cassette collection.

Her cheap, blue-cloth, three-ring notebook fell out on top of the math, biology, American lit, and world history books. It was the kind you wrote on in ballpoint pen: tic-tac-toe games, interlocked initials, and assorted doodles. Janie opened the cover. The back of the flattened milk carton stared up at her.

FLOWER DAIRY
"The dairy that cares"
100% whole milk
one half pint

She unclipped it.
Turned it over.
Jennie Spring looked up at her.
The 800 number was like a dart being thrown into her eyes. I could call, she thought. I could ask—
But what could she ask?
All the questions were unthinkable.
Besides, what would it do to her parents to find out their very own daughter was calling the authorities to announce she had been kidnapped? Her mother, who had spent the day baking a special cake, and was too tired to consider going to the bank . . . her father, who would come home from soccer full of victory or deflated by loss.
Janie picked up her phone.
She dialed 1.
She dialed 800.
She dialed 346-72—
She was gasping for breath.

With two digits to go, she hung up.

She missed the phone. It clattered, slid off the bed, and hit the floor with a crash as loud as trains colliding.

But her mother did not yell upstairs to see if Janie was hurt. Up here it was the world crashing in; downstairs nobody had heard a sound.

All right, get a grip on yourself, thought Janie. The dictionary is right: These are inspired by a demon. You have to destroy the demon. Or maybe it's just premenstrual syndrome.

Except she had never previously had trouble before, during, or after her periods.

I will think about Reeve now, she ordered herself, glaring at the inner demon. I will think of kisses and love and dating.

But she thought of Jennie Spring. Of parents somewhere in New Jersey who missed their little girl so much that all these years later they were still hoping, hoping by the thinnest thread they would somehow find their Jennie again, and Jennie would be safe, not murdered or raped or abused—

—*or happy and ignorant with another family.*

This, thought Janie, must be what heavy drugs are like: hallucinations whether you want them or not. Temperature-changing, personality-changing doses.

This time she dialed Sarah-Charlotte.

Busy.

Then Adair.

Adair had total-phone and gave Janie twenty seconds of her time. She was on the phone with

Pete, who, she said, seemed to be on the verge of asking her out. "Then what'd you answer my call for?" demanded Janie. "You might have cut him off at the moment he got the courage together."

"Normal persons," said Adair, "can never resist a phone call." She disconnected to go back to Pete.

Janie called Michelle, who did not have total-phone.

The phone rang twice. Somebody picked it up. Janie disconnected immediately.

Rude! thought Janie. Why'd I do that? Because I can't talk to Michelle about anything. If I told Michelle about Reeve, the next day the whole school would think Reeve asked me to marry him. If I told Michelle about the milk carton, the whole school would know that I actually believe I was kidnapped. Guidance Department would hear the rumors. They'd summon my mother from her Bloodmobile. *Your daughter's hoping you're not her parents; your daughter is planning to call the FBI on you; your daughter is living in a sick, twisted, perverted daydream in which . . .*

Her body vibrated with a queer, frightening energy, as if she could have run all the way to New Jersey to that shopping center.

What if I can't get this horrible idea out of my brain? she thought. What if it sits there, and grows, like some terrible egg, splitting open and turning into something real?

CHAPTER

6

In separate cars, the Johnsons, the Shieldses, and the Sherwoods drove upstate to the football game.

"Please let me drive," Janie begged her parents. "Sarah-Charlotte's family is letting her drive because she needs highway practice. And Reeve gets to drive the whole way."

"Reeve's had his license an entire year," said her father. "And Sarah-Charlotte's been practicing longer than you have."

"I've never driven on the highway," said Janie. "Please, please, please? This is a perfect day to start. Lots of sunshine, no rain, no ice on the roads, no summer-people traffic."

"All right," said her mother nervously.

"Certainly not," said her father.

Old times. Progressive mother, conservative father. Janie waited for the debate to commence, and for them to meet in the middle. They would probably let her drive part of the way.

"Oh, all right," said her father. "I keep not wanting to believe you're going to be sixteen soon. I don't like the year sixteen."

Janie giggled and took the keys from her mother's hand. Her parents clicked their seat belts firmly, as if to say, *we're sure going to need them this time*. "Have faith," said Janie reproachfully.

"Take off the parking brake," said her father.

"I was going to, Daddy, you just didn't give me time." She backed perfectly out of the driveway.

Not only did Reeve come out his door in time to see her drive, but so did his older sister Lizzie.

Lizzie was not one of Janie's favorite people. Lizzie had occasionally baby-sat for Janie in the past, but not because she liked kids. Lizzie rarely did anything except for the money. Lizzie was supposed to be safely in law school now, being as brilliant there as she had been in Princeton. Janie did not consider Lizzie's absence a loss to the neighborhood. How annoying to see Lizzie home. It would certainly tense Reeve up.

Even from the far end of the driveway Janie could see how straight Lizzie's spine was; how intense her face; how determined her jaw. It seemed unlike Lizzie to come home for a mere football game; Lizzie was opposed to frivolous waste of time. Lizzie was also opposed to Reeve, and had been all their lives.

But there was a silver lining to this. Reeve would be very eager to go off with Janie.

She wanted to wave to Reeve but was not coordinated enough to change gears, aim the car, miss the curb, and wave all at the same time.

Reeve did not act as if Lizzie had crushed him yet; he leaped around like a demented boy cheerleader, signaling with both arms and screaming syllables she could not hear.

"Look out for that car up there," said her mother.

"You're following too closely," said her father.

"Please," cried her mother, "not over twenty-five."

They were gripping the seats, the belts, and the armrests with white knuckles.

"How'm I doing?" said Janie happily. She loved driving. The power of it! Even diluted by her mother and father's panic, power filled her body. She, Janie, controlled destination, speed, passing, radio volume, and stopping time. She felt as if she had been born to drive, as if car designers had molded the driver's seat just for her. She loved checking the rearview mirror and watching the brake lights ahead of her and reading the route numbers on road signs.

For Janie it was a perfect hour and a half.

However, Reeve and Sarah-Charlotte, permitted to drive normal speeds like real drivers, had arrived first. When the Johnsons reached the designated parking lot for tailgate picnics, Sarah-Charlotte and Reeve stood on the pavement shouting, "You'll never be able to park it!" "Jinx, jinx!" "Try steering, woman!"

She parked perfectly. "So there," she said to her parents.

Her mother said, "This is an excellent weight-loss program. I'm sure I'm five pounds thinner than I was when I left home."

"You'll put it all back on eating your own picnic," said her father, dragging out the leg of lamb, the wine, the wild rice, and the sheet cake with the footballs. And that was just what the Johnsons had brought. Reeve's mother had a ham and Sarah-Charlotte's mother had all the classics: potato salad, coleslaw, macaroni salad, and fried chicken.

The weather was wonderful: sweater weather. In the shelter of their three cars, they ate till forced to rest their stomachs. "We'll need a tow lift to get us up into the stadium," joked Janie's father, who had had lamb, ham, and fried chicken.

Janie's mother played with the aluminum foil hiding the sheet cake while Lizzie discussed the constitutional law cases she was now analyzing. "If Lizzie laughs at my cake . . ." Janie's mother whispered to her.

"Or at you," Janie murmured back.

"We'll murder her," breathed Janie's mother.

"But then we'd need a lawyer," whispered Janie, "and we'd just have gotten rid of the only one around." They giggled.

Mr. Sherwood thought the kids should go away and explore the campus before dessert, thus giving the adults some peace.

"We're not babies anymore," said Sarah-Charlotte irritably, "needing our diapers changed and our bottles heated."

"No, but you talk a lot more," said her father, "and we'd like our own conversation without you, okay? But I still love you. Kind of." Sarah-Charlotte made a face, claiming this lukewarm parental love meant she deserved her own car, insurance paid and gas supplied, of course.

"Uh huh," said her father dryly.

Reeve turned to his sister, grinning. "Come on, Lizzie," he teased. "They want the kids to leave. So they can have a mature conversation."

"I am the only one here who will bother with a mature conversation," said Lizzie. "They just want to gossip." She took a chicken leg, leaned back, and said to Janie's father, "Your turn, Frank."

Janie tried to imagine one day calling her friends' parents by their first names, failed, and fled with Reeve and Sarah-Charlotte. They wandered around the campus, talking about what college would be like ("If I get in," said Reeve gloomily) and how they yearned to live in dorms and be away from the confining rules of their parents.

Janie was lying.

College terrified her.

There was nothing she wanted less than to live on her own. The harsh glass-and-steel dorms the freshmen had did not look as if they could ever be home to anybody. They looked like cages for loneliness. Imagine five thousand freshmen you had never met.

Reeve said, "My parents and Guidance think I should take a postgraduate year, repeat some of my high school subjects to get better grades, and then go on to college."

"How humiliating," remarked Sarah-Charlotte.

"You're supposed to tell me nobody would notice," said Reeve.

"Of course they'd notice, it would be like staying back," said Sarah-Charlotte, who was not sensitive. "Jordan Feingold and Linda Lang stayed back in second grade and I never see them without remembering that."

"How comforting," said Reeve.

Janie wanted to hold his hand. The one whose thumb had drawn itself so lightly down her nose, bumping over her lips, landing on her chin. But she could not tell if Reeve was interested in this or not. He was full of energy. She and Sarah-Charlotte were sloths compared to Reeve, stumbling in his wake.

They had excellent seats: six rows up, left of center. Janie mostly watched the cheerleaders, who were heavy on gymnastics. They had tiny trampolines and were endlessly catapulting off each other's shoulders. She particularly liked how one tiny cheerleader with flowing golden hair stood on the palms of a boy cheerleader who could hold her easily at his own shoulder level.

With some ceremony, Mrs. Johnson opened her sheet cake for admiration and cut it up to serve during the second quarter. They ate it with their fingers, getting icing all over themselves and licking their fingers clean because nobody had remembered napkins.

"Lemme have another piece," said Reeve, nudging his hipbone into Janie's.

"You had two already," she said. "I'm cold, don't move away."

He didn't move away. She cut another square for him and something gave her the courage to feed it to him, bite by bite. His lips and tongue touched her fingers with every bite. Neither of them saw the second half of the game. They were both startled to find it had ended. People were on their feet. Sarah-Charlotte was saying, "We won, you two. You want me to write out the details so you'll feel as if you were here?"

Sarah-Charlotte spent the night at Janie's.

They rented movies—comedies they had seen before and knew they'd like. Sarah-Charlotte grilled Janie at great length about Reeve, analyzing the leaf pile and the football game. "He loves you," said Sarah-Charlotte.

"You don't have to sound so irritable about it," said Janie.

"I didn't want to be the one left behind. Pete asked Adair out and here's Reeve literally eating out of your hand, and who is there for me? Nobody." This led to the always pleasant activity of ripping apart the personalities of boys who had displayed no interest in Sarah-Charlotte.

They slept late and their sole activity in the morning was reading the Sunday comics.

Monday morning in Spanish the teacher passed out information on a winter vacation trip she was chaperoning to Spain. "Anybody who wants to may go," she said. "First come, first serve."

"Oooooooh, let's," breathed Sarah-Charlotte, nudging Janie.

"If you have any thoughts of going at all, and you don't yet have a passport, you need to apply immediately," said the teacher. "It can take months. You need your birth certificate and another piece of identification to get one."

The bank is open today, thought Janie.

In English they got back their corrected essays. Janie got a B. "Sweet sense of humor," Mr. Brylowe wrote, "although not what I had in mind." At the top of the page he had circled *Jayyne Jonstone*, adding, "Janie, you having an identity crisis?"

At lunch Janie got a wrist flick from Reeve, nothing more. She thought: He's not ready, or maybe not even thinking about doing anything public. She wondered what stages you went through to reach the moment when you could speak to each other in front of your friends, or refer to each other, admitting, *I like him.*

"I thought he was going to ask you out," said Sarah-Charlotte sadly. "Janie, he's so adorable with that moppy hair."

"He needs a decent haircut," agreed Janie. She didn't commit herself to anything more. She opened her lemonade carton. The rest opened their milks. She looked at Jason's milk. There was a different child on the carton.

A boy.

Nobody mentioned him.

Nobody referred to Janie's claim last week to have been the kidnapee. As far as Janie could tell, nobody even remembered; not even Sarah-Charlotte.

Adair had everybody's attention, having skipped first-period class to go to the Motor Vehicle Bureau for her driver's test. Flushed and proud, she displayed her brand-new license. Everybody politely agreed that she was recognizable in the photo, although she was not; nobody ever was.

Adair wanted to show off her driving skills. Everybody, she insisted, had to be passengers in her car and go to the mall that afternoon. "You coming, Janie?" said Adair, more excited than Adair ever allowed herself to be. Janie had not known that Adair's smooth finish, shiny as shellac, was an achievement Adair worked for.

But Janie wanted to go to the bank, not the mall. She said by way of excuse, "I'll have to call my mother and ask."

"Janie, you're still not allowed out by yourself?" teased Jason.

"Her mother is the strictest woman on earth," said Sarah-Charlotte.

"How come?" Jason wanted to know. "What terrible history do you have, Jane Johnson?"

CHAPTER

7

She came home to an empty house. Mondays were hospital volunteer days for her mother. Her father would be coaching at the middle school until dark. When did the bank close?

Janie went into her mother's study. She had a vague idea of finding the key to the safe deposit box and going to the bank herself.

The desk had two deep file drawers. The upper one was crammed with volunteer-related materials: all her mother's committees, boards, and causes. Girl Scouts (that was ancient history), Hospital Volunteers, Literacy Volunteers, Nature Conservancy Board (Janie had never even heard of this one), Parent/Teacher Association . . . in alphabetical order, the files went on and on. There was something very reasssuring about those files: full of her mother's time and energy and caring. Paper memories of meetings, fund-raisers, and suburban routines that made the world a better place to live in.

The frightening daymares of last week had not come back. Janie was more irritated than anything else, wanting to set aside the milk-carton idea; driver's licenses and passports were of much greater importance. If she could just see the birth certificate, she could extricate herself from this dumb idea. In the bottom drawer would be files marked Bills, Income Tax, Insurance Forms.

The bottom drawer was locked.

She found the lock strangely frightening. Her mother did not lock up jewelry, nor silver. So why lock a file drawer? What robber would care about her last-year's bills?

No key was mixed in the pile of paper clips and index tabs lying in the shallow pencil drawer.

Upstairs, Janie changed into old jeans and a sweatshirt. She found herself checking corners of her room for reassurance: Yes, her T-shirt collection was intact. Yes, her bumper-sticker collection was still in its shoebox. Yes, her Barbie dolls still lay silent in their carrying case at the back of the closet.

I should put them all in the attic, she thought. They're clutter. I want my room to be more streamlined than it is.

The attic.

Boxes and trunks. Whenever they went up those dark stairs for things like Christmas decorations, Janie would ask what was in those boxes gathering dust in the corners. "Junk," her mother always replied. "Someday we'll toss it."

Now it occurred to Janie that her mother—everybody's favorite chairwoman—was supremely organized. If she had intended to "toss it," or if it really were junk, it would never have gone into the attic; she would have donated it to the Salvation Army.

Janie opened the door to the attic stairs.

Cold drafts, like winter coming, sifted down on her face like dust.

The roof creaked.

She climbed the stairs. I've never been up here alone, she thought suddenly. If I ever needed my old Halloween costumes, or my last-year's winter boots, Mom went up for them.

At the bottom of the stairs, the draft made the door shut.

Janie whirled when it slammed.

Her heart was pounding.

She crept down the stairs, in case it was an intruder.

Of course it was nothing.

Putting books on each side of the door to hold it open, she went back up.

The attic was poorly lit. The previous owners had remodeled the kitchen, dining room, and bathrooms, but nobody had done anything up here, not even dust. The attic felt as old as time. Eaves ran down toward the floor and made dark corners.

On most boxes, her mother's neat handwriting spelled out the contents. *J—handmade sweaters.*

Janie smiled and opened that one. The sick scent of mothballs filled the attic. Child's sizes, long outgrown. The sweaters reeked of memory as well as mothballs: a Christmas-tree sweater, cream and green, brought back third grade in a rush of sound and color. That Christmas they'd gone to Disney World. She'd needed the sweater; it was cold in Orlando that year. She remembered sitting in the whirling teacup with her parents, clinging to her father's chest, shrieking in delight and dizziness. Billy Wadler, a big, mean fourth-grader, had teased her mercilessly all January about wearing a Christmas-tree sweater.

Billy Wadler had grown up into a really terrific guy. He took out his aggressions in sports now and was nice to girls. Sarah-Charlotte had always yearned for Billy.

Janie smiled and closed the cardboard box. It was hard to interfold the four cardboard pieces as neatly as her mother had done. She coughed from the moth balls.

The next box said *F—ski boots.*

Her father. Frank. She hadn't known her father skied. Maybe they'd do that this winter. She'd ask. She wondered why he'd given it up. Too expensive? Too dangerous?

The whole quest was beginning to feel quite silly. What a good thing that she had not explained anything to Sarah-Charlotte, nor asked anything of her mother.

Up against the very back, hidden by two neatly stacked rows of cardboard boxes, old jigsaw puzzles, and fishing equipment, a black trunk had been pushed. She remembered the fishing-equipment birthday. Her father had gone out twice, but he was not the fisherman type. He disliked solitary sports. How disappointed he had been when his only daughter preferred a social life to soccer!

She was smiling when she reached the black trunk. Probably my baby clothes, she thought. If Mom saved all my sweaters, I bet she saved all my baby clothes.

It was such a nice thought. Janie could hardly wait to see them: eensy, sweet, smocked things she loved to look at in stores.

The trunk was big and cheap, the sort you bought from Sears or Montgomery Ward, metal trim now tarnished.

It was locked.

A label was taped to the top. A single letter was written on it.

H.

Who was H? Her mother was Miranda, her father Frank, she was Jane. None of the four grandparents had been an H either.

An old Christmas-tree holder, three splayed feet and a cup for the trunk, lay gathering cobwebs. Janie wedged its metal foot behind the long, narrow lock-plate of the trunk and yanked.

The lock broke.

How old it must be, thought Janie. It's rusted through.

She lifted the heavy lid carefully, tilting it back against the wall. The trunk was filled with papers and photographs. She was immediately bored. Old school reports, old term papers, old fill-in-the-blank maps and quizzes. Somebody named Hannah. She had never heard of anybody named Hannah.

How could an unknown Hannah merit this stack of attention? Janie felt irritable and coughed again from the dust and the mothballs.

Beneath a sixth-grade report on "The Beginning of Mankind: Mesopotamia," and a sheaf of mimeographed maps where Hannah had wrongly penciled in *Germany* on France, was a school photograph. Janie recognized the cardboard folder immediately: the kind that offered your parents six different purchase agreements, so many wallet sizes, so many eight-by-tens.

She flipped open to see what Hannah looked like. A pretty girl—perhaps twelve or thirteen—looked back at her. Sweet, blond, mild. The kind Sarah-Charlotte would refer to as a Used Rag Doll. "Not much stuffing in that one," Sarah-Charlotte liked to say of girls who were short on personality.

The dust was annoying Janie's lungs. It would be the pits if it turned out she had a dust allergy along with a milk allergy. How would she survive in this world if everything made her choke and cough?

From behind all the papers a little piece of fabric stuck up.

White cloth.

Tiny dark polka dots.

With hands of ice Janie plucked at the material, shifting the layers of school papers until she could pull it up.

It was the dress on the milk carton.

CHAPTER 8

For supper her mother had made a pot roast, with potatoes, turnips, onions, and a rich, dark, thick gravy. Janie had no appetite. The smell, which ordinarily would have brought her into the kitchen with her father, moaning and clutching at things, pretending starvation and deprivation, made her ill. She ate nothing.

"Janie, honey, don't you feel well?"

She shook her head. "I'm fine."

"What can I fix you, then?" said her mother. "Would you rather have soup and toast?"

"I'd rather have a McDonald's cheeseburger," said Janie. "I hate this old-fashioned, heavy-duty, mom-in-the-kitchen stuff with gravy." It was like stabbing her mother. She had to look away from the hurt on her face.

"My child of this century." Her mother struggled to make a joke out of it. "Pizza Hut is better than my chicken potpie, and a McDonald's cheeseburger beats out my pot roast."

Her father had seconds and then thirds to make his wife feel better. He complimented her extravagantly on the texture and flavor of the gravy. Janie knew they were waiting for her to take the initiative and apologize, so they didn't have to tell her to.

"How was school?" said her father.

"Oh, you know. School."

Her father drew a long breath. "We had a great practice. I can't wait for the next game. Lincoln Middle School graduated all its competition, so we ought to slaughter 'em. Janie, I want you to come. You haven't seen my team play yet. How about coming to tomorrow's game?"

He was as eager as a little boy to show off his team.

I could put an ad in the Sunday classifieds down there in New Jersey, thought Janie. What could I say? *Need more details. Describe Jennie Spring. Who is Hannah?*

But that would give those New Jersey parents hope that I exist. That I am out here, and I miss them, and I want them.

I exist. But I don't want different parents.

I like everything exactly the way it is.

How can I have a mother—or a father—or both—that I don't miss and don't want? Am I some kind of monster?

But now that I know they're out there, how can I leave them hanging? Never knowing that I'm fine?

Why am I fine? How could Mother and Daddy do it? Are *they* monsters?

Her father pulled her thick red hair back into a ponytail and brushed his face with it. "Come on, Janie," he coaxed. "I need you out there cheering. Bring a crowd. Make all those high school kids come and yell for us."

"Daddy, don't pull my hair like that." She tugged herself free. Now she had hurt her father as well.

He loves me, she thought. How could love arise from a crime like kidnapping?

"There's a great movie on tonight," said her mother. "Want to watch it with me?"

"Can't. Too much homework." Janie left the table, clearing her entirely clean plate. She went up to her room, shutting the door firmly. She tried to put her parents out of her mind, but Janie was peace loving. The little fight stuck her like needles.

She calmed herself going through her clothes, deciding what to wear tomorrow. There was an Honors Breakfast. The marking period had ended; the first quarter was over. It seemed to her they were shooting through fall, rocketing toward winter, that Christmas would have arrived before she had even gotten her winter coat out. She was in the mood for an entire new wardrobe. She wondered if her mother would take her—

—shopping.

Shopping.

Memory struck like an ax. It was the clearest daymare yet, complete with dialogue.

They were clothes shopping.

(*They.* Who were they? She could not quite see them. But she could hear them.)

"No, you can't have that, Jennie, you've got loads of hand-me-downs."

"But Mommy—"

"Not now! Can't you see I'm busy with the twins?"

"But Mommy—"

"No! You don't need a patent leather handbag."

Jennie stomping off by herself. Finding that store with those high, swiveling stools. Sitting at the counter. Swinging herself in circles. Pushing herself by the edge of the counter.

The counter was a pale, greenish-flecked Formica; the napkins popped out of a little stainless steel box.

The woman with the long, shiny hair sat next to her.

Bought her a sundae.

Toward eight o'clock her father knocked on her door. "Kitten? May I come in?"

"Sure."

Who was the woman? thought Janie. My mother downstairs? Another wife of Daddy's? The shopping mother? She called me Jennie. And I answered. It was my name.

Her father entered tentatively, as if he did not know her or the room. "Something wrong, honey? Why are you mad at us?" He was a big man, lean, able to have seconds on gravy without a thought. He had gone gray early, but lost no hair. The mass of gleaming silvery hair was distinguished.

She said evenly, "Why would you think that?"

"Because you are. You're hostile and mean. What's going on?"

"You tell me." She wanted to force answers out of him, but she did not want to ask the questions. They screamed at each other, and theirs was not a screaming family. Janie could not remember when she had thrown ugly words at her parents.

But in the morning she had to rush to school for the Honors Breakfast: jelly doughnuts, orange juice, and coffee supplied by the Parent/Teacher Association for anybody with the grades. It was dumb and embarrassing but nobody ever missed it. You didn't get the rounds of applause for a B average that you got for playing football, nor the spotlight for a terrific term paper that you got for the jazz band. You had to settle for a jelly doughnut and one line in the newspaper listing.

Reeve was there.

"Reeve?" said everybody, staggering around, clutching their hearts, running to the principal to double-check the honors list. "This is Reeve? *Our* Reeve? Reeve whose arms have never been weighted down with those paper and cardboard things known as books?"

"Drop dead," said Reeve. But he was grinning.

Janie beamed at him. "Reeve, I didn't know you were doing so well," she accused him. "You made me think you were going to have to repeat your entire academic career."

Reeve shrugged like a little kid. "I wasn't sure I could get the grades," he admitted to her. "I never tried before. Grades are what Megan and Lizzie and Todd do, not me."

"Mr. McKane," Sarah-Charlotte said to the principal, "did Reeve pay you off? Or is he just a misprint on the honors list?"

"Reeve studied brilliantly," said the principal. "Reeve is becoming a fine, fine student, indeed, just like—"

Don't let McKane say *just like his sisters and brother*, thought Janie. It will ruin it for Reeve. Let this be Reeve's, not some spin-off. "Just like me!" she said, striking a center-stage pose and flinging her vast quantity of red hair around.

"Oh, yeah," said Sarah-Charlotte, "you who sneak in here with exactly point one percent above the minimum. Reeve, if you're going to imitate anybody, imitate me." She flirted madly with him, seizing his wrist and beginning to dance wildly. Reeve grinned.

Joyfully, the PTA president announced that it was time to sit down. "What a fine, fine chance for all you brilliant young people to get to know each other better and find new friends," she said, trying to make them talk to people they didn't want to talk to.

She had no success.

It appeared that nobody wanted any new friends. With much grumbling they tried to shuffle place cards and sit with their old friends. PTA mothers intervened. Janie ended up at a table with all juniors and seniors, none of whom she knew. She looked yearningly for somebody to switch with, but Reeve had landed with seniors who were giving him a ritually hard time for having joined academic ranks, and Sarah-Charlotte was lost in the crowd.

"Introduce yourselves to the person next to you," caroled the PTA mother. Janie was very glad her own mother had been president when Janie was in middle school, and she had been spared this humiliation. She knew who the PTA president's kid was just by checking out the hunched shoulders.

"Hi, I'm Dave," said the boy next to her dutifully.

"Janie," she said.

"Tell me about yourself," dictated the PTA mother, as if they were memorizing lines from a play.

"Tell me about yourself," repeated Dave.

"Well, I was kidnapped at age three from a shopping center in New Jersey . . ." Janie panicked. Had she said that out loud? Had those words really fallen out of her mouth? No, surely not!

"Just the basics," said Dave teasingly. "This isn't an autobiography for advanced comp. Where were you born, who are your parents, how long have you lived in Connecticut, that kind of thing."

The room shifted and the table slanted. She wondered why the coffee did not spill, why the doughnuts did not slide to the floor. Dave blurred when she tried to face him. Parents and Hannah, kidnaps and cars, drove through her eyes and crashed at the back of her brain. "I—uh—play tennis a lot."

"She's afraid of you," said a senior girl. "Gee, that's pretty neat, Dave. You're not only an honor student, you're a Big Bad Wolf."

The older kids all dropped their voices an octave. "You're biiiiiggg," they drawled, pointing at Dave, "and you're baaaaaad, and—"

Janie's head cleared. She said, "I faint every morning if I don't have all the jelly doughnuts in sight. Somebody quick pass me a jelly doughnut."

"We ate all the jelly doughnuts," said the girl. "You have to have a plain one."

"She can have mine," said Dave. "Look. Chocolate icing. Now there's an energizer." He held it out of reach, so she would have to make an effort—touch his hand—lean toward him.

Dave was interested in her. *Interested.* That world of dating and movies and the backseats of cars. If she smiled back in the right way, one thing would lead to another. She wondered if Reeve was watching. If she flirted with Dave, would Reeve be angry? Jealous? Would he decide to speak up and claim her before Dave did? And Sarah-Charlotte, was she watching?

Janie looked more carefully at Dave, to assess his personality and appearance. She became aware that Dave had asked her another question. "Ummm," she said. "I—um—wasn't listening."

"I said," said Dave very clearly, "where are you from? I just moved here last year from Colorado."

She knew he was trying to start a real conversation. That being from Away—having First Impressions of This Part of the Country—was a classic opener.

But I don't know where I'm from, she thought. Or who I am.

The breakfast was over. Half the people at her table had already left. One of them was Dave.

Sarah-Charlotte came over practically hissing. "Janie Johnson, you could at least talk to the guy. What's the matter with you these days?"

"I don't know," said Janie. She tried to imagine herself telling Sarah-Charlotte the kidnap stories.

"It's not like he's asking you to sleep with him, you know," said Sarah-Charlotte.

Janie did not know why Sarah-Charlotte had to go so far in her plans for Janie. One kiss with Reeve and Sarah-Charlotte had decided Janie had a sexual history.

"And he was so adorable," said Sarah-Charlotte. "I never noticed him before. It's odd how you can be in school with people you never see."

School that day was a queer and floating place.

Janie filled her spot. She talked, wrote, wended her way from hall to class. But she was a mind floating in an ocean of confusion, battered against milk-carton photographs and attic trunks.

It was raining again that afternoon, so Reeve gave her a ride home. She wanted him to say *I love you*. Or, *Let's go to a movie*. Or, *Don't be friends with Dave, be friends with me*. But Reeve just poked the radio buttons endlessly, dissatisfied with every station. She wanted him to kiss her again and she wanted him to suggest it, or start it.

"I can't make small talk," she said. "Breakfast was awful. It was like filling out a form."

Reeve laughed. "I loved it. All the girls flirted with me."

Why did he say that? she thought, utterly miserable. I don't want to be the one who's jealous! "Dave kept asking me questions I didn't know the answers to."

"He asked where you were born," said Reeve. "You couldn't come up with that?"

"Reeve, I don't know the answers to questions like that."

Reeve moaned. "That sounds like my philosophy class. I hate that kind of thing. Don't you start it."

"Reeve, if I tell you something, will you keep it a secret?"

"The Johnsons have secrets? I don't believe it."

"I don't believe it, either. That's half the problem. I can't tell if I'm going insane, or taking drugs in my sleep, or if . . ."

"If what?"

But it was too preposterous to say. Especially to Reeve. He more than anybody would find it absurd: he knew the family too well.

"Janie," said Reeve loudly, as if saying it for the tenth time, "we're here. Get out."

She stared at him. Who was he? Had she ever seen him before? Her fingers fumbled for the handle. Her hands were stiff and numb, as if she were going into rigor mortis.

She remembered leaving the stool. The stool that could only be in that shopping center in New Jersey. Remembered hopping down from that green counter and leaving that half-eaten vanilla ice cream sundae. Remembered somebody taking her hand, saying, "Let's go for a ride now." She remembered herself laughing . . . delighted . . . and going.

I gave up my real family for a sundae? thought Janie Johnson.

*　*　*

She crossed the shrub barrier between their driveways. Both her parents' cars were there. She walked slowly, rain pouring on her hair and her face. Inside the side door she scuffed the bottoms of her wet shoes on the rubber mat.

Her mother had made a pot of coffee. Janie could smell it, filling the house like breakfast and warmth. She walked into the kitchen. It was like a child's scene built in a shoebox for second grade. Her father pouring milk in his mug; her mother filling the sugar bowl; the clock chiming; the snack they were having—a Pepperidge Farm cake—defrosting on the counter.

I will go mad if I don't find out, she thought. If I'm not already mad.

Still dripping from the rain, clinging to her book bag, Janie said, "I want to know why there aren't any photographs of me until I'm five. Even if you didn't buy a camera until then, you would have had a baby portrait done. I want to know who Hannah is upstairs in the trunk. I want to know why you won't let me see my birth certificate."

9

A silence as long as some lives.

Janie thought she might fall over.

Her father's hand was molded to his coffee mug. Her mother's hand stuck to her spoon.

Janie could not step closer. She could not run away.

The demon had seized them all in his daymare.

Her mother sank very slowly into a chair. Her father very slowly raised his chin to look into his wife's eyes. Like puppets they nodded.

Screams rioted in Janie's skull.

She gripped the book bag as if she planned to throw grenades.

In syllables that dropped as softly as notes on a flute, her mother said, "Hannah is your mother, Janie. We are not really your parents."

No! cried Janie's soul. No no no no no—

"We are your grandparents. Hannah was our daughter."

Janie dropped the book bag. "Is that all?" she

cried. She flung herself onto her mother. "Is that all? I thought—oh, Mother, you just can't imagine what I thought." She could not stop repeating herself. She hugged her mother ferociously, feeling the strength of wrestlers in her arms. "Oh, Mommy, that's all it is?"

We're related, it's okay, she's all but my mother, there's no daymare, no nightmare, no demons, Hannah just had an illegitimate baby and it's me and that's all there is to it.

Her father came up behind her, gave her a ponytail, and pulled her backward by her red hair. His hug was also the hug of wrestlers, hanging on to her, as if they were in danger of falling over cliffs. She leaned on him, letting the horrible cliff of kidnapping out of her mind.

"We love you, honey. You are our daughter. Just not legally and biologically. We don't have a birth certificate for you. So we don't know what we're going to do about your passport and your driver's license and things like that."

"Who even cares?" said Janie. She found she was sobbing. Her hair was wet, her coat was wet, her cheeks were wet. Her mother peeled away the outer layer of Janie's clothing. "I'll fix you a snack," said her mother. She patted Janie, as if to dry her by hand. Her mother's teeth were chattering.

"Food solves all," agreed Janie, laughing through tears.

"The old Johnson family motto," said her father.

Janie pulled away from them. "But I'm not completely a Johnson, then."

81

"Nobody here is a Johnson," said her father. "It's a long story, Janie."

All three were breathing hard, as if from a long jog in the cold.

"Let's sit on the couch together," said her mother, forgetting snacks. "So we can hug. I've rehearsed this in my mind a thousand times, but now that we're here, I've forgotten my lines."

They sank together in the big velvet couch in the living room, Janie in the middle, a parent holding each hand. She was so tired from the assault of emotion she could hardly hold her head up. She rested against her father's shoulder.

"Our name is not Johnson," said her father. "It's Javensen. We've never come across the name anywhere else. It has a Scandinavian sound, but we really don't know much about my family."

Javensen, thought Janie. I like it, she thought. It's better than Jayyne Jonstone. Jane Javensen.

"Your mother and I . . ." Her father's voice staggered, like clumsy feet. "I guess I'd better say, your grandmother and I."

Janie shuddered. "No. Don't say that." She put a hand against his chest as if to trap those words.

"We'll call us Frank and Miranda, then," said Janie's mother.

And the story her parents told, line by line, agony by agony, was so sad that Janie wept for them.

Frank had a degree in accounting and Miranda had a degree in medieval literature. Frank went to work for IBM in marketing, they got married, and a year later a baby girl was born. They named her

Hannah, which meant full of grace. Hannah laughed and cooed and was happy her entire childhood.

"Hannah was my whole life," said Janie's mother. Her eyes fastened on a past Janie knew nothing of.

I'm your whole life! thought Janie, jealous and angry that somebody had come before her.

But Hannah had been an unusual child. Janie frowned when they described Hannah. She could think of no girl who even slightly resembled Hannah. Hannah had never wanted to do the things other girls did: she didn't play with dolls or ride a bike. When she was a teenager, she didn't care about boys or getting a tan or the radio. She worried about right and wrong. From the time she was very small, the inequities of life horrified Hannah. How could her family have so much and the world so little? Miranda could volunteer for a cause, do whatever a committee could do, and return home happy to a good dinner. Hannah never felt she deserved dinner.

"Hannah was beautiful," said her father, "in a haunting sort of way. Hannah always seemed to be looking at something else. In another age she might have become a nun and spent her life thinking of God. But we were not a religious family, and I don't suppose she even knew what a nun was."

The oddest thing was happening: Janie was falling asleep. The sleepless nights worrying about the milk carton and whether to dial the 800 number had caught up to her.

"Do you know what a cult is?" her father asked.

Janie shook her head, bumping his shoulder.

"A cult is a religious group with exceedingly strict rules for the people who join it. The Hare Krishna movement swept America like a prairie fire in the sixties and seventies, Janie. It attracted young and old, hippie and conservative, East Coast and West Coast. And it attracted Hannah. She met a group of young people who told her that if she became a Hare Krishna, she would be purified. It would no longer be her fault she had so much, because they would not let her have anything. She would be saved. When she was sixteen, she fell on her knees and begged to be allowed to be one of them."

Janie could picture none of this.

"They were scary people," said her mother. "They wore bright yellow robes, the men shaved their heads, they carried bowls and begged. You saw them everywhere in cities, in airports, chanting and demanding money. But where we tried to be honest with Hannah, saying, 'Nobody knows why some people starve and some people have everything,' the leaders of the cult had answers for all her questions. And what Hannah wanted, in the end, was a set of answers and a set of rules."

Yellow robes made her think dimly of *National Geographic* photos. But it evoked no memory.

"Sixteen therefore is a terrifying age for us," said her father. He tried to laugh. "That's why we're having such a hard time with you, Janie. We have to give up part of you. Let you drive; maybe take the trip with the Spanish class; go off to college; make your own decisions—but Hannah's decision! It ruined our lives and hers."

"Why didn't you tell me before now?" Janie asked.

Her mother was shuddering violently, from her teeth to her knees. "Because we were so afraid you'd want to find your mother, or maybe your father, and get sucked up in that cult, too! I can't go through that again. I can't lose another daughter. Janie—please—"

They need me, thought Janie. They need my comfort. "I wouldn't do that to you. You won't have to go through that twice. I promise."

Her parents kissed her on each side. Her mother took both her hands now and held them against her cheek, as if in prayer. "We tried everything to get Hannah out. We took her on long vacations, we sent her to live with my cousin in Atlanta, we tried traditional church. But she went to California to join the temple commune. There was nothing we could do. The law wasn't on our side, Hannah wasn't on our side. The cult even had armed bodyguards to keep parents like us from snatching our children back."

Snatching children, thought Janie. To think I actually thought Mommy and Daddy had snatched me! She could no longer keep her eyes open, but let herself doze against her father's warmth.

"We wrote continually," said her mother in a strangled weep, "but Hannah rarely wrote back. The few times we were allowed to visit, she seemed dulled. Like a silver spoon that needs to be polished. She spoke only when spoken to. All her responses were memorized. Our beautiful Hannah had stopped smiling forever. 'I'm very happy here,' she would say tonelessly, like a mechanical object."

"I was still with IBM," said her father. "I was transferred frequently. We sent Hannah every address change. Whenever I went on a business trip, I mailed her postcards. I suppose I thought I could entice her back into the world with pictures of waterfalls in the mountains or castles in Europe."

Janie tried to remember California.

Her mother whispered, "We *were* good parents, Janie, we *were*! We never knew what we had done wrong, or why she rejected everything we ever taught her. We tried everything to get her back. We sent police, we paid the cult off, we tried to debrainwash her when she visited. But she wanted to be in the cult. She was like a very tall, docile toddler: she simply obeyed her Leader; her mind was strangled. We wept on her birthday and that was all we had of Hannah."

Her father described the passage of years in which Hannah led a weird enclosed life with harsh, incomprehensible people.

"We got an official letter telling us she had been wed to a man in the cult. That was all they told. Not even his name. Then one day," said her mother, "the front door opened. I was making pound cake for the Women's Club bake sale. I was in the kitchen adding six eggs to the batter and the beaters were whirling. I had added the first four. I remember that so clearly. I had two eggs to go. And there stood Hannah—holding you by the hand."

Her parents sat up. Janie was amazed by this mutual physical response of the emotions. Even their posture knew the worst was over. Her father leaned forward, resting an elbow on his knee and cupping his chin, so he could look at Janie. Her mother's voice lightened. She ran her hands through Janie's red mane, held both Janie's cheeks, and kissed the tip of Janie's tilted nose. "You were such a beautiful child!"

I was a resurrection for them, thought Janie. Hannah reborn.

"You were her little girl, by the man who had been chosen as her mate by the Leader."

"Mate?" repeated Janie. "What an animal term for the love between husband and wife!"

Her mother didn't hear her. "You had no clothes except the clothes you were wearing. I had the best time taking you shopping! We bought sweet little socks with ribbon trim, and the cutest little jacket with bunnies on it and a tiny little beret. It was so adorable against your red braids. You had the best time! You had never had so much attention. I suppose in the cult you were in some kind of day care. You often referred to the other children and asked about them."

Those twins, thought Janie. The spilled milk. It was just day care.

"We gave you your own bedroom and you thought that was the most exciting thing that ever happened."

"You know what would be exciting now?" said

her father. "Dinner. I am absolutely starving. Nothing builds an appetite like trauma."

Janie giggled. She felt warm and toasty and complete.

"Let's nuke the leftover pot roast," he said. "Are there any potatoes left, Miranda?"

"No, but I can make instant mashed if you want them, Frank."

"I love instant," said her father.

They went into the kitchen, as if leaving the bad parts of the story behind in the living room. Good things happen with hot food, thought Janie. "So, go on," she said when the pot roast was nuked. "Hannah came in the door and you bought me tons of clothes and then what?"

"Well!" said her mother excitedly. "Hannah had realized the cult was a terrible way to bring up her little daughter. So she escaped! She didn't even like you near the windows for fear the guards of the cult would be there, peering through the curtains. The second night of celebrating Hannah's return and your existence, we realized the cult could find us just as easily as Hannah had, because of course we had always sent our forwarding address."

Minutes ago Janie had been incredibly sleepy. Now she was incredibly hungry, eating as if she had never known food. Her hands shoveled the meat into her mouth. She felt like an animal. Her parents saw nothing. They were a tag team, rotating speeches.

"IBM knew all about Hannah and the cult because I was always flying west trying to extricate

Hannah. They not only transferred me immediately, they got us into a hotel that night under assumed names until they could pack our belongings for us. My senior vice-president even sold our house through a power of attorney for me so the cult wouldn't find our names anywhere. We had all mail forwarded through the company, never to our house."

She had no memories of the West Coast. This cult with its costumes, capes, and rituals. The woman and man who were Hannah and her designated mate. No memory of a cross-continental flight. Three years old. Wouldn't you remember planes and trains, cars and overnights, even if you were only three? thought Janie, disappointed.

Janie Johnson . . . a name to disappear under. A name without personality. Without trace.

"You had the best time, Janie!" said her mother.

For the first time Janie saw clearly how old they were. Much older than her friends' parents. And more tired, too. More used.

Hannah, what did you do to them? thought Janie. How could you have thrown them away like yesterday's newspaper? Your own mother and father, who tried so hard to give you everything; to get you back?

"We were fleeing, but you were in heaven, Janie, bouncing all over the place." Her mother painted a happy little Janie in the new houses—buying new clothes—teaching her to swim—Hannah standing blank-eyed—packing boxes never unpacked before the next flight—yet another different driveway—Janie dancing like a water sprite.

"But even though we did all we could," said her father, "Hannah eventually wanted to go back to the cult."

This time Janie entered the daymare willingly, as if it were a hallway down which she could walk if she chose. She felt that down that corridor she could find Hannah, find California, remember that nursery school. The laughter of children rang in Janie's head. Then something different—*a man's laughter—big and chesty—and she knew herself held in the air by this man—a red mustache— she was tugging the mustache and he was nibbling Jennie's fingers—she could even feel its texture, bristled like a paintbrush, same color as her own braids—she could remember the braids, remember the way the rubber bands yanked when—*

"Hannah was addicted to the cult the way some people are addicted to heroin. When Hannah insisted on going back, we let her." Her mother's voice grew urgent. "She wanted us to keep you, Janie. I've always cherished that. She loved you very, very much. You have to know that."

In the windows her mother's red geraniums still bloomed. Their lives in the sun were probably happier than Hannah's. Her mother's hands covered Janie, patting, needy. "She gave you up so you could have a real life. Your mother gave you the gift of freedom, Janie. It was the only gift she had to give. She left you with us when she went back to the cult."

Shortly after Hannah left, Frank and Miranda

had realized that the cult would want the little girl. Not to mention the father, whoever he might be. Hannah had no strength. One interrogation and she'd tell the cult where she had left her daughter. Their attorney advised them to change their name. Javensen was too unusual. So they had taken Johnson.

—"We moved several times in one year," said her father. "Looking back, I suppose it was irrational. But whenever we let you out in the yard, we'd panic. So we kept finding a new yard. You loved it. You were always giggling, always the center of attention. It took you a while, but eventually you switched to calling us Mommy and Daddy."

Her mother beamed: a smile like the sun.

If I hadn't come to live with them, Mom would never have smiled like that again, thought Janie. *I am that smile.*

"And then we made the most painful decision of all," said her mother. "We never wrote to Hannah again. Our only daughter. Your mother. We never sent her an address. We never again telephoned on her birthday. We never chose and wrapped another Christmas present for her. We let her vanish into nowhere so that we could keep you safe."

They were no longer at the table, no longer eating. They had all gotten up, their bodies desperate for comfort. They were hugging each other, an oddly rocking trio. *"Oh, Mommy!"* said Janie. They cried together.

Her father did not weep, but then he never did;

he got tight; the muscles bunching in his jaw, no doubt also in his gut. Janie hugged him separately, and her father hugged her back, with affection so deep she could hardly bear it.

They are my mother and father, she thought. They raised me. They love me. I love them. Mother and Daddy are all I have, and all I want.

CHAPTER
10

She woke up as if attacked, ripped out of sleep.

Her body was drenched in sweat, and her thin nightgown clung damply to her skin.

Monsters and hideous, evil, sucking things scattered in her brain. She lay in the dark, clinging to the satin hem at the top of the blanket. *Just a dream, just a dream.*

She wanted to get up and get a glass of water. Find another blanket. Turn on some lights.

But she was caught in an old childhood fear of things under the bed: the silly fear that kept her even now, at nearly sixteen, from sleeping with her toes hanging off the edge—something might nibble them, drag her down.

Slowly she curled tighter and tighter under the covers, bracketing her spine with her pillow, protecting her heart and soul with tucked-in knees.

It was a nice story they had told last night. But what about the Springs? What about the milk carton? Hannah was real. The trunk in the attic full of her geography papers proved it. But the milk carton was real. Jennie Spring was real and so was that 800 number. New Jersey was real. And that shopping center.

I remember a friendly kitchen with lots of kids. I remember shoe shopping. I remember . . .

Memories swirled dimly. She held herself still, trying to pull them in, like a fisherman with a reel. The cult did not sound like people who took their nursery-school class shopping in malls for shiny white shoes.

The white apron? Was it Hannah's? Why did she remember a white apron and not yellow robes? California and cults should make a deeper imprint on a child's memory than a sundae and a swiveling stool.

Janie's made-up versions slipped and slid like cars on ice; they crashed into what few dim memories she had—or had created. But one thing was true and certain: the dress in the attic matched the dress on the carton.

In the dark of her bedroom an idea misted in her brain like fog: dank and sour and thick.

Had Miranda and Frank Javensen, their minds warped from losing Hannah, decided to replace her? With a new little daughter?

Had they gone for a drive? In the heat and the sun and the dusty wind? Had they landed in a shopping center in New Jersey? Had her mother—a different, younger mother—twirled on a stool beside a little girl named Jennie Spring? Bought her with nothing more than ice cream? Taken her home forever?

A real kidnapping.

Her dear, sane, good parents.

Janie's notebook faded in and out of her brain like the shadow of a migrating bird, with the flattened milk carton clipped to the cover. She could show them the milk carton. She could say, "I know the truth."

But then what?

She didn't want the truth to be true any more than they did.

She wanted to be their daughter, too.

Janie lay awake the rest of the night, sifting her brain, finding nothing certain.

In the morning, they had breakfast together. This was unusual. Her father normally left for work before Janie got up; her mother liked to be solitary in the morning and sipped coffee alone in her bedroom, reading the morning paper, while Janie had a glass of orange juice and a croissant.

They were as nervous as strangers waiting to have their teeth drilled. They drank orange juice as if it were spiked with cyanide. They buttered toast and abandoned it.

How had her parents slept? Janie wondered. Were their hearts on Hannah this morning? And my heart, thought Janie, where is my heart?

Janie was too exhausted for speech. In her head the daymares clamored for attention: toddlers in high chairs pounding spoons on the tray, laughter richocheting off kitchen walls, car doors slamming. The faces of her mother and father at the breakfast table seemed to crawl over and through the daymares.

Her father set his untasted coffee next to his untouched toast. "Janie, honey, are you all right?"

"Sure, Dad."

Her father's smile was pasty and peculiar. "You don't look as if you slept."

"No. There was a lot to think about."

"Do you have any questions?" her father said nervously.

She had a million questions. But they would answer in lies and she could not bear it. Her father—whom tax clients and soccer teams adored and respected? Her mother—who cared so passionately about the hospitals and the illiterate and the schools? Telling lie after lie after lie because in fact they were criminals?

Perhaps they don't even know anymore, she thought. Perhaps for them, too, the daymare has blended with the daydream, and the truth is lost.

"You and I should spend the day together," said her mother. "I'll phone the school. I'll cancel my meeting in Hartford."

"No, I have an important test. Anyway, I want to talk to Sarah-Charlotte."

She would never tell Sarah-Charlotte. She would never tell anybody. What words were there? *My parents are insane. They lost a daughter and kidnapped another, except that they probably didn't; I'm probably their granddaughter with a demon inside.* "Go to your meeting. I'll see you at supper."

Her father said, "Maybe it's best to try to keep things normal. Regular schedules. That sort of thing."

Normal, thought Janie, choking back hysteria.

Her mother turned into a whirlwind, gathering papers while she snatched up clean stockings from the drying rack, telephoning another board member while she wriggled into her crimson suit. She always looked so authoritative in that suit.

Her father wanted to kiss her good-bye. His arms seemed to hang inside his jacket as if they had been stapled there. He had a hard time lifting them toward Janie. Her father, whose perfect coordination came from years and years of sports. This morning his silvery hair hung on his forehead like a grandfather's, not a father's.

He's afraid I won't love him as much, thought Janie. But I do. I don't care what they did. I love them just as much. How can that be?

"I love you, honey," said her father desperately. "I'm sorry about—about all of it. But—"

"I love you, too." Janie tacked on her brightest smile, allowing him to leave. He hugged her, but she did not hug back, and he knew it and was afraid.

"Janie," he said, "we did the best we could. With you and with Hannah."

"I don't care about Hannah," said Janie, which was certainly true.

Her mother came rushing back. "Do you think this pin looks good?" said her mother anxiously, touching the silver brooch she had fastened to her scarf. Her mother didn't feel comfortable with pins. She was always sure they had drooped or turned themselves backward. "It looks fine," said Janie.

She looked out the window. Pouring again. What

was with all this rain? At least she could ride with Reeve this morning instead of waiting for the bus. "Good-bye, Daddy," she said, forcing herself to hug him. "I hope your meeting is good, Mom."

Her father said, "You'll telephone me at the office if—if you're upset or anything, won't you?"

Outside in the rain, Reeve honked his horn.

"Have a good day at school, sweetheart," said her mother. "I—maybe I should stay by the phone in case you want to call. Or—I could call you from Hartford."

"Mom," said Janie, "everything's fine. Don't worry. See you later." She grabbed her coat, her books, her bag lunch with its nonmilk drink, and flew out the door. Reeve had given up on her and reached the end of his driveway. Screaming, she ran after him. "Reeve! Here I am!"

He saw her, grinned, reversed, and waited for her. "Thought you took the bus after all," he said. "Did you sleep late? You look frantic."

She laughed hysterically.

"That's just how I feel," he agreed. "Here I make a hit by getting on honor roll and the very next day I don't finish my homework and I have to go make an ass of myself with an oral presentation in English."

"I wish we could cut school," Janie said.

"Okay. Let's," said Reeve. "There's nothing I want in that building."

They were heading into town; they were on the overpass of the interstate. Janie said, "Get on the highway, then. Head south."

Reeve's jaw dropped. "You serious? Janie of the sweet, obedient personality wants to cut class?"

"Yes. Turn. Hurry up. You'll miss the entrance."

Reeve got on the highway and turned south.

The windshield wipers clicked rhythmically. The rain thudded metallically on the roof. Reeve turned the radio up louder; they were listening to KC-101 Rock. Janie had never heard KC-101 at this hour; she was always in school.

The miles went by.

They passed a turnpike rest stop and gas station.

Their speed dropped. They were in rush-hour traffic. A thousand cars throbbed around them.

"We can't turn back now," said Reeve, waving his watch. His grin tested her, to see if she was serious.

Buddy, thought Janie, you don't know how serious I am.

"We're officially late," said Reeve. "We go to school now, we have to get late passes from the vice-principal and they telephone our parents."

"It doesn't matter," said Janie. "We're going to New Jersey."

11

They spent two hours on the Connecticut Turnpike. Janie read every blue and white highway sign as if it were immortal literature and she was going to be tested.

On the New York Thruway they paid a toll and turned north for White Plains, where they headed for the Tappan Zee Bridge and crossed the Hudson River. The river was very wide and flat, the same gray color as the sky. A single barge floated downstream.

All that water, thought Janie, and no traffic on it. She stared at the apartment buildings and houses on the riverbanks and pretended to choose a place where Jayyne Jonstone would live. Jayyne Jonstone. She had planned Jayyne to be mysterious and sensual and full of flair.

She had always thought of mysteries as exciting curtains, to be tugged aside to reveal intriguing pasts. But her mystery was sick and vicious. Was she even now driving on the very road that

Frank and Miranda Javensen had driven down when they made their horrible decision to replace Hannah? Had they ever talked about it? Out loud? Ever said to each other, "Why don't we kidnap somebody?" Or had it just happened of its own accord, without plan, and then somehow had seemed right to them, instead of hideously, evilly wrong?

"Janie," said Reeve, "it's impossible."

Janie held up the milk carton.

"I see the milk carton," said Reeve. "But that isn't you. How could you recognize you after all these years?"

"I don't recognize me. I recognize my dress. Reeve, this dress is in the attic! In Hannah's trunk."

"Come on, there must be a trillion polka-dotted dresses that little girls wore once. My sisters probably wore that stuff. So big deal."

"It is a big deal, Reeve."

She could feel that Reeve wanted to drive a hundred miles an hour and was angry with the traffic and the law for keeping him back. "And who could this Spring family be?" demanded Reeve. "Maybe it's a conspiracy the Springs dreamed up to destroy your mother and father. They'd go to prison, you know, if they really kidnapped you." Reeve looked right at her. "Which they didn't," he said.

Prison. Another dark and vicious word. She had never seen a prison, except on TV cop shows. Her mother—stripped, searched, locked up, and tormented?

Mommy! Janie's heart cried.

But out loud she said calmly, "Okay, I've been studying this map of New Jersey." She was glad driving took so much of Reeve's attention. He did not have much turnpike experience; the heavy, truck-filled traffic kept Reeve's eyes ahead, or on the mirrors, but rarely able to meet Janie's eyes. "It's a good thing that gas station was stocked with maps. We want to get off in seventeen more exits, and then turn south. The town where the shopping center is will be halfway between—"

"What are we going to do when we get there?" Reeve demanded.

She said nothing. She did not know yet.

"Janie, how'm I going to explain to my parents where we've been?"

"Why do we have to explain to anybody? Let's say we went—um—just driving around—killing time—we felt like skipping school."

Reeve said uneasily, "They'll figure we found a motel room or a nice private beach. They'll figure it's sex we wanted, not getting out of a test or an oral report."

Janie swallowed. Normally a natural, unnoticeable task, swallowing had become almost an athletic event. It's too cold for a beach, she thought. She pictured herself and Reeve on hot sand, nothing but a string bikini between them. She said, "It's a long way. New Jersey is a much bigger state than you think it is."

A double truck passed them, spraying such a puddle of water over the windshield that they were blinded. For a moment they were as isolated as if

102

they were trapped in a tin can. Reeve turned the wipers up to high. The water was whacked away. "Though anybody less interested in sex and romance than you would be hard to imagine, Janie. You're a little scary. You're like this hard, sharp, pointed *thing*."

He doesn't like me, thought Janie. I'm in the car with my best friend. I guess he's my best friend, and not Sarah-Charlotte, because it's Reeve I've told. He wants not to be here. He doesn't like this person in his passenger seat. "I've got to find out," she said.

"Why don't you just ask your parents?"

"Reeve, what am I supposed to say? 'Daddy, stop telling me these cute little stories about Hannah's childhood. Admit you kidnapped me.' It would hurt their feelings."

Reeve laughed hysterically. "But Janie, if they did kidnap you, who cares about their feelings?"

"I do. They're my parents and I love them."

Reeve said, "I think we're a little confused here."

"Wouldn't you be?" demanded Janie.

They drove on and on. New Jersey seemed to last forever. Signs for Philadelphia began to appear. That's Pennsylvania, thought Janie. She knew nothing of Philadelphia except the Revolutionary War and the Constitutional Convention. Now I'm sliding into a time warp as well as a kidnapping, she thought. I've lost my parents, I've lost my name, I'm losing my century, too.

Reeve found the silence intolerable. He began telling her more than she had ever known about his own childhood. About how Lizzie and Megan were so impressive in everything: music, sports, academics, even housework. How Lizzie and Megan were virtually an opposing team of two in the Shieldses' household, each determined to get all the blue ribbons. How Todd, born the year between them, struggled endlessly to be seen and heard in that aggressive sandwich of sisters. How Reeve, born years later, had merely stared at all these superachievers, doing nothing much himself but making the occasional Lego building or turning a TV channel.

I lived next door to them, she thought, and I hardly noticed. How much does anybody ever notice?

She found herself thinking of Sarah-Charlotte, who had not noticed any change in Janie. Janie's life had collapsed. Sarah-Charlotte nevertheless telephoned each night, giggled each lunchtime, and did not notice.

They had long since lost KC-101 on the radio. Reeve tuned endlessly, trying to find a station he would like as well. When he had nothing more to say, he turned the radio up so loud they could no longer hear the rain.

"Say something," said Reeve.

"It's this exit," said Janie.

Reeve turned to look at her for so long she was afraid they'd go off the road. Briefly, this seemed quite reasonable. Forget finding answers. Abandon life instead.

He expected me to say something about his childhood, she thought. About all those painful confessions he just made. But I'm too deep in my own painful confession. I am a bad person. I was a bad daughter. Because a good person, a good daughter, would have noticed she was being kidnapped! She would have remembered her real parents. She would have wept and sobbed and fought and tried to get home. She wouldn't just trade them in. And certainly not just for an ice cream sundae.

"Janie, what if we find these people? These Springs?"

Her mind was so cluttered with confusion she had not actually planned to look for the Springs. She had planned to walk through the shopping center and see if it triggered any memories. See if she could find that stool in front of that green Formica counter. See if she could remember, instead, Hannah and the cross-country flight.

Reeve got off the New Jersey Turnpike.

We're here, thought Janie. Fear seemed to throw water up over her eyes, the way the truck had thrown it on the windshield, and she was canned inside her fear.

"Spring is an unusual name," said Reeve. "There might be only one Spring family in the phone book."

There was an International House of Pancakes at the side of the road. Reeve swung suddenly into their parking lot, and they jolted in the air as he leaped over the sidewalk. "Let's have pancakes and think about this," he said. "They could be home. We might find them. What are you going to say when you ring the bell? 'Hi, there. Am I your daughter?' "

Janie shivered. I don't want to be their daughter. I want to be Mommy and Daddy's daughter.

Reeve parked, opened his door, circled the car, opened her door, and took her hand. She still had her seat belt on and it jerked her back in. When Reeve undid the seat belt catch, Janie began to cry.

"Don't do that," said Reeve, horrified.

"What else is there to do?" She imagined herself at some unknown doorway, some unknown woman answering it—would it somehow be Hannah?—a twelve-years-older Hannah?—would there be other children? But years had passed. The high chairs would be gone.

She crumpled against his chest. They stood in the rain, Janie hugging his middle. He was more solid than she had expected, and she could listen to all his inner parts: his heart beating in double thumps, his lungs filling in rhythm with hers.

"Janie, the thing is, I think they would call the police. That's what I would do. Janie, think! Can you imagine the scandal? If you made all of this up, they're going to put you in a mental institution and give you counseling and shrinkage forever. Your parents will be wiped out. Wiped, Janie. Off the map." Reeve tilted back from her and held her face up off his wet jacket. He slid his hands back along her cheeks until his fingers were tangled in her hair. "How would they face a whole town, all those soccer parents, all those volunteer ladies, and say 'yes, our daughter accused us of kidnapping her?' " He looked into her eyes and she thought: He loves me.

She could actually read it in his eyes. But she did not know what kind of love it was. Compassion? Neighbors? Older brother?

Reeve tried to lead her into the restaurant. She remained rooted to the spot. "So," he said, trying to kid around. "Not in the mood for pancakes? How about a cheeseburger? I see golden arches in the distance."

Janie shook her head.

"Janie, what if you're right?" His voice was shaking. "The police won't let you go back to your parents—well—to Mr. and Mrs. Johnson. They'll—" Reeve sucked in air. "Something will happen, I don't know what. Social workers and newspaper reporters and TV cameras and—"

"We won't actually go to the door," said Janie. "We'll just drive by."

Reeve pointed to a telephone booth across the street at a Mobil station. They pivoted to face it, staring as if at the Great Pyramid in Egypt. Then they got back in the Jeep. Reeve circled the ugly A-frame restaurant with its slick brown roof. Janie was gasping for breath. Her head hurt savagely. Her hands hurt even worse. She looked at them, to see if she had slammed them in the door or something, but they were clasping each other so hard she was trying to snap her own bones. She made herself let go. Reeve crossed traffic and pulled into the gas station. He maneuvered until he had her passenger door right in front of the phone booth.

She prayed the phone book would have been stolen.

But it was there, hanging in a metal case by a metal cord.

Her life, her soul, her history, her genes.

She got out of the car and stood again in the rain. The rain was a known quantity. It seemed as safe as Reeve's chest.

Then she went into the booth and looked up Spring.

There was one listing, and one only. How ordinary it sounded. How suburban and middle class.

Spring, Jonathan Avery . . . 114 Highview Avenue.

She walked into the gas station. A youngish man in need of a shave and a good weight-loss program sat in filthy blue coveralls behind a greasy table and leered at her. She said, "Would you please tell me how to get to Highview Avenue?"

For a moment she thought he would refuse. That would be a sign, wouldn't it? That she was not meant to know. That even total strangers knew better than to let Janie Johnson near Highview Avenue.

But he said, "Long way, baby. South on this road about two miles, left on Mountain Road, it's down Mountain somewhere. Read the street signs. Easy to miss. Good luck."

She got back in the Jeep, dripping wet. Reeve turned the heater blower up high to dry her off. "South on this road," she told him.

"Janie, I think we should go home." He was white and pinched. "I thought when you said skip school together you really wanted to do something neat with me, Janie. I didn't know you just needed a chauffeur for something like this. I don't want to be part of it. No matter how much you want to know, I don't want to know at all! I was thinking that you—" He broke off.

He was thinking that I liked him, she thought. I do like him. I adore him.

Her head pounded on and on. She had never had a headache like this. Hammers and spotlights behind her eyes.

She touched the cuff of his shirtsleeve where it stuck out of his jacket and then very softly, nervously, touched the skin of his wrist. She traced his wrist on each side of his watchband. She wanted to kiss his wrist, and the golden hairs that almost invisibly caught in the spiral tension of the band. If he had not been driving, she would have yanked him toward her, kissed him forever.

Reeve said, "Janie? In the leaves? That day?"

But the part of her not suffering a headache and the part of her not aching with love was reading street signs. "There's Mountain Road, Reeve. Turn right there."

They got caught behind a school bus.

"What time is it?" said Janie, frowning.

Reeve held up his wrist for her but she couldn't read upside down. "Two o'clock," he said. "They must get out early here."

Two o'clock in the afternoon! she thought. We won't get home till after dinner. What am I going to tell my parents? They'll be so mad at me! They'll never let me—

She had to take her hand away from Reeve's

wrist and put it over her own mouth to stifle hysterical laughter.

The yellow school bus stopped once. Stopped twice.

The third stop was for Highview Avenue.

The one hundred block.

It was a development, perhaps twenty years old: mostly split-levels with identical front bay windows opening into pleasant yards and thick shrubs. Each house had a two-car garage, and most had hedges between them. The similarity among the houses was rather comforting, as if this were a neighborhood where you could predict what would happen next, and be safe.

It had momentarily stopped raining. Enormous puddles attracted the children as they leaped off the school bus. The boys jumped square into the puddles, soaking their sneakers, splashing mud on the girls, who screamed happily and threw things, like lunchbag apples they hadn't eaten.

Reeve stopped the Jeep while the children crossed the street.

Two boys, about sixth-graders, went to number 114.

Spring, Jonathan Avery . . . 114 Highview Avenue.

The boys had red hair. The color of Janie's.

She subtracted the years she had been gone. Had they sat in high chairs in that kitchen once while she spilled milk on the floor?

We had a dog, thought Janie. *A big dog. Yellowish. I used to hug the dog and she'd lick my face and my mother would yell at me. Honey was the dog's name.*

The front door on number 114 began to open for the redheaded boys. They were not latchkey kids. Somebody was home to welcome them. The inner wood door was bright red. A hand reached to push open the storm door. Janie covered her eyes and sank down in the seat. "Drive past, hurry up, Reeve, drive past."

There were too many children dancing on the sidewalks, wild with release from school, to drive fast. He drove about ten more houses and parked the car. "The woman who opened the door has red hair, too," he said.

"It's not true!" said Janie. She could not tell if she was whispering or screaming. Her skull was vibrating as if dentists' drills had gone crazy inside her. "I refuse to have it be true. Reeve, take me home. You were right. We have to make up a good lie, we can't tell anybody about this."

From the other direction came a second yellow school bus. It stopped quite close to them at the intersection of the two-hundred block. It was the high school bus. A handful of teenagers got off, none interested in each other, going their separate, bored ways.

A tall, skinny boy, from whose right shoulder swung a nearly empty book bag and a pair of enormous sneakers, headed toward them. "Now those are serious feet," said Reeve admiringly. "I hope the rest of his body grows to fit. Look at the size of those feet."

Look at the red hair, thought Janie Johnson. *That's my brother.*

The boy never saw her; he checked out the Jeep, and he checked out Reeve, but was not interested in the passenger. The sneakers, hanging by tied laces, banged his chest as he walked. She turned very slowly in the seat and watched him. He crossed the street; he glanced in a newspaper cylinder. He put his right hand on the fender of a parked car and used it for leverage to toss himself over a hedge. He leaped into the air to touch the sagging, leafless branch of tree. The branch snapped back and jittered. It began to rain again, as if the twig had punctured the cloud.

The boy went in the front door of number 114.

The drive home took forever.

They had not known there was this much traffic in the entire world, let alone New Jersey to New York to Connecticut. Reeve was exhausted. His hands gripped the wheel, his eyes darted around. He would never have admitted it, but the pressure of the racing cars, the huge trucks inches away, the endless turnpike entrances where cars nudged his fenders, trying to squeeze in, visibly frightened him. Neither one had driven anywhere but their own safe, slow corner of the world.

Janie kept looking at his watch.

"Should we call them?" she said nervously. "Tell our parents we're fine, but we're going to be late?"

Reeve said, "Well, if you can think of anything to say to your parents, go ahead and call. I'll stop at a McDonald's on the Connecticut Turnpike.

But I know what my parents are going to think. They're going to think you and I went to a motel to learn about sex. My sister Megan did that with her second boyfriend. His name was Philip. My mother still gets a fever whenever she hears the name Philip."

They crossed the Hudson River and hurtled on toward Connecticut. There seemed to be no way out of the traffic; it had a nightmarish, eternal quality; as though they might be doomed to race wheel to wheel with the rest of the world, never reaching any destination.

Janie said, "A motel." She tried to think in terms of romance. Or at least sex. Both were certainly easier subjects than kidnapping and another set of parents. Spring, Jonathan Avery, whose family consisted of at least three brothers.

And a missing daughter.

The radio brought traffic reports. Highways they had never heard of were jammed for miles; bridges they had never crossed were impassable; alternate routes with preposterous names were suggested.

Reeve's hands suddenly loosened on the wheel. "It's not too late," he said.

"For what?"

"For the motel."

The speed in their lane never slowed. Nobody had ever heard of the fifty-five mile per hour limit. Anybody driving fifty-five would have been crushed beneath the wheels of a thousand automobiles, each flattening them a little more, till there was nothing left in the road but the metallic gleam of a car that drove too slowly.

She could touch him in places she had never touched another human being. She could lean on a chest not covered by layers of wet jacket and buttoned shirt. "I don't think I could concentrate," she whispered, wetting her lips.

"Maybe if I concentrated enough for both of us?" said Reeve.

CHAPTER

12

They were in Connecticut. They passed the beautiful suburbs from which commuters went daily to New York City, then hurtled through the ugly mill towns and smog-rimmed cities that lined the shore farther east.

Reeve took an exit.

"Are we out of gas?" said Janie.

Reeve shook his head. Down the exit ramp they went, and the sudden release from traffic and noise was like taking off heavy coats. Janie felt thin and easy again.

Reeve turned left at the stoplight, went back under the turnpike, and there in front of them was a motel.

The motel was nasty: flat-roofed, crouching rows of cheap pinky-yellow doors. "How will you pay for this?" said Janie.

"I have my father's American Express card."

They both registered. Reeve wrote in his tall, cramped handwriting "Reeve Shields."

She took the pen and froze up. *I have no name. I am not Janie Johnson nor Jayyne Jonstone nor Jane Javensen nor Jennie Spring.*

The clerk saw her hesitation and gave her a sick, sly grin.

She wrote "Jane Johnson."

The clerk turned the registration card around and read the names out loud. "Jane Johnson?" he repeated, smirking. "Big imagination, lady."

Reeve's fist came out, terrifying them all.

The clerk leaped backward.

Reeve grabbed the key instead of decking the clerk. His hand locked on Janie's arm and he hauled her outside. They stood panting in the smoggy, rain-laden air of industrial Connecticut. She said, "Reeve. I can't."

She expected an argument but she got none. He just nodded. He looked for a while at the cement blocks that were peeling with old vanilla-colored paint, and the rain puddling through rusted gutters. They both knew if he had gone to a different sort of place, with a safer, richer, cleaner feeling, they could have. Would have.

Reeve shrugged. He stuck the key in the motel mailbox and they went back to the Jeep.

Janie said, "When we do it for real, Reeve, it won't be like this."

"When?" said Reeve softly. His long face seemed thinner than ever, and his open mouth a stranger's. Then his wonderful joyful grin split his face, and he turned back into Reeve, her trusty, rusty next-door neighbor, and he grabbed her waist and swung her around, then stood very still, kissing her.

It was a full-length kiss; she felt him down the entire length of their bodies, through their clothes, through their coats. The ice of her fears was replaced by a shimmering heat. A heat that was Reeve.

"I don't think I can drive," said Reeve when they were in the Jeep.

"Well, I can't, not in this traffic."

"You want driving experience, take it."

Neither of them wanted driving experience. It was another experience altogether they wanted. "Start the motor," said Janie.

"Believe me, it's running," said Reeve, and they giggled desperately.

"What time is it?" said Janie. She blew a long puff of air upward, lifting her hair off her rain-wet forehead.

"Late," said Reeve. "I don't know why we worried about New Jersey calling the police. If we don't get home soon, our parents will be the ones to call the police." He touched her hair (hair he had yanked a million times when he was nothing but an annoying brat next door) as if she might refuse him permission; as if he were touching gold. He took a breath so deep she thought his rising chest might split his shirt, and then he fell back against his own window instead of against her.

"Reeve, we registered. There's going to be a bill. It'll come through on your parents' American Express next month. Your mother will talk about Megan and Philip," she said. She gripped the seat belt when she wanted to be exploring him.

"I don't think my mother wants to go through that a second time," said Reeve. "I always planned to keep it a secret from her when it was my turn. Why does my turn always come so much later than Lizzie's and Megan's and Todd's turns?"

They managed to talk. He managed to drive. Neither of them, radio addicts though they were, remembered to turn on the radio. The car was filled with rhythm and rock of their own thoughts.

The journey that had lasted so long rushed by toward the end. They fell silent. He took their exit. Drove through their town. Passed the houses of their friends, the streets of their childhoods.

"Janie," said Reeve suddenly. His voice shocked her in the quiet of the car. "Your parents have been my parents, too. They raised me as much as my own. Whenever Lizzie and Megan and Todd were driving me nuts, I'd be at your place. I haven't figured out the truth in this New Jersey stuff, but Janie, we can't jump to conclusions."

"Oh, okay, sure," said Janie. She was sick with nerves. "Just because they have my hair and I remember the dog Honey and it's my dress on the carton, we won't jump to any conclusions."

"Okay, so the conclusions are there staring us in the face. The fact is, your parents are going to be there staring us in the face in about a minute. What then, Janie?"

I promise, you'll never have to go through this a second time. She herself had said that. And meant it. But Janie had not quite realized she would have to go through it, too. And not just once. All her life she would be part of whatever had happened in that shopping center in New Jersey.

Reeve drove up their hill.

The lights of both the Shields and Johnson houses were on from attic to cellar, as if their parents had been searching for bodies in hidden corners.

"This is it," said Reeve.

"I don't want to go in alone."

"I don't want to go in at all."

But there was no need to go in.

Four angry, screaming parents came out instead.

CHAPTER
13

It was wonderful to be yelled at. It was so parental.

Her mother's face, taut with worry and rage, was a mother's face. Her father's hands, rigid with wanting to shake her by the shoulders till her teeth rattled, were a parent's hands. They loved her. Parents who loved you bothered to get mad.

Once years ago, furious at Sarah-Charlotte, Janie had stomped on Sarah-Charlotte's glasses and purposely broken her friend's retainer. When her parents saw the pink plastic splinters on the sidewalk, Janie thought they would kill her. And that time she cheated on the math test in sixth grade. That occasion was memorable first for the screaming, and second for the failure her parents had insisted she get for the entire marking period, even though the teacher was willing to forgive Janie. And of course the time she and Sarah-Charlotte, aged ten, decided to see whether it was true what they heard at a slumber party, that you died when you had Coke and aspirin at the same time. The time her mother said Janie was old enough now to do her own laundry and ironing, and Janie replied, "Forget it. You do it or I'll stay dirty."

Ah, the yelling.

They're my mother and father, Janie thought. That's why they're so mad. That's what mothers and fathers do.

"Janie! How could you do this! No matter how upset and angry and confused you were, you know what a telephone is."

They yelled and she basked in it; it was like sunshine in summer, seeping into her pores.

"You could at least show some remorse," shouted her father, "instead of smiling at the driveway!" while next to him Mr. Shields bellowed, "Reeve! How could you have done this! Did you know about this Hannah nightmare? And yet you purposely the very next day whisked Janie off so her mother and father had to go through it again? That was horrible of you! What kind of person are you?"

Those people in New Jersey are just people in New Jersey, thought Janie. I don't want them and I don't care about them. "I'm sorry, Mom," she said. "I'm sorry, Daddy. We decided to cut school so we could talk. We just drove around for hours. Nothing happened."

"Nothing happened?" repeated her father. He had aged. Tonight he was indeed a grandfather. Lines creased his cheeks as if he had slept on a pile of books. The distinguished hair was just a tired gray. "We paced the floor for hours in complete panic. Wondering if you'd ever come back. Wondering if you'd bother to let us know. And you dare tell me nothing happened?"

Reeve simply stood still, waiting it out. Boys did that.

Janie's mother, exhausted from worry and relief, burst into tears. "Janie, why didn't you tell us at breakfast you were that upset? Why did you lie and insist everything was fine? We would have done anything. Hannah ran away like that! I thought you were—"

"We weren't running away," interrupted Reeve. "We were talking. That's all. I know we should have called and said we were fine, but we didn't. I'm sorry. Everything's fine."

"You have a very strange concept of the word 'fine,' " said Reeve's father. "Let me assure you, you are not fine right now. You are about to get the punishment of your life. Get in the house."

Reeve and Janie looked at each other. They won't let us see each other again, thought Janie. I won't be able to ride to school with him. His father will ground him the rest of senior year. "But Reeve helped me," said Janie desperately. "I needed him and he was there."

The yelling stopped.

Their parents stood quiet and limp. Nobody had touched. Nobody had reached out to forgive or hold.

Reeve's mother surprised them all. "Then I'm proud of you, Reeve," she said huskily. "Frank and Miranda told us about Hannah and the cult.

It must have been a terrible shock to you, Janie. It certainly was a shock to us. Now that you're back, and we know you're safe, I suppose I can admit that helping Janie work this out was much more important than a day at school."

Reeve changed gears as fast as a race car. "We could talk about it again tomorrow, Janie and I," he suggested brightly. "It was probably enough shock to skip school all week."

"I think not," said Reeve's father.

Inside the Shieldses' house, the phone began ringing. "It's Megan," said Mrs. Shields. "Or Lizzie or Todd. We called to see if you had run away to one of them."

Reeve stared at his mother. "Megan's in California," he said.

The adults nodded. "So is Hannah, presumably," said Janie's father, looking old enough for canes and nursing homes.

"Oh, Daddy!" cried Janie, hurling herself on him, as if she were three years old instead of nearly sixteen. *But I'm not nearly sixteen. Jennie Spring on the carton has a different birthday altogether. She's six months younger than I am.* "I'm not going to join some creepy cult. I'm not running away. Daddy, I'm sorry," Janie linked arms with her elderly father and trembling mother.

Her parents made a sandwich around her. They were both taller, and she was tucked between them like a child. "We don't know where Hannah is. We don't even know if she's alive," said her mother, weeping afresh. "Cults went out of fashion. I haven't seen any Hare Krishna in years.

Hannah could be wasting away on some forgotten commune in California or she could be a bag lady in Los Angeles. Who knows?" Her mother rocked Janie back and forth, but she was really rocking herself, or baby Hannah. "You promised last night we wouldn't have to go through this again," said her mother. "And twelve hours later it began."

Her mother's voice changed to begging. *Don't hurt me, Janie.* "Janie, please," said her mother. Raw, bleeding.

Mr. and Mrs. Shields and Reeve went in to tell Megan, Lizzie, and Todd that the lost had been found.

Janie helped her parents inside. Consoled them. Made promises. She knew that she would never talk about New Jersey to them. They could not endure it.

New Jersey. What a nice, catchall phrase for the mess that had erupted in her life. It rounded up the chaos into a neat rectangle below New York, leaning onto Pennsylvania and waving out over the Atlantic Ocean. "I'm sorry," she said again. She began crying harder than her mother.

And her mother, being motherly, recovered somewhat. "Don't cry, honey. It'll be all right. I love you. Daddy loves you."

Her father stared at the wall, his jaw clenched to prevent weeping. His eyes were saddest, laden with grief he chose not to shed. And whether he was thinking of Janie next to him, or Hannah gone forever, she did not know.

Think of *me*, Janie thought. *I'm* your daughter.

*   *   *

The nightmare came like mud: thick. Oozing filth. The mud hung on to her feet and her brain. It was filled with reaching hands and cackling laughter. Car wheels spun in the mud and fingers pointed. Janie ran but her feet did not move. Trucks tried to run her over, and when she screamed for help, her parents were busy with other things.

She woke up. The bed was drenched with her sweat. What time is it? thought Janie, groping for the clock. If only it could be dawn, so she could go downstairs and start coffee, be done with this horrible night.

But it was two A.M.

She wept briefly. Her mother had said, "We love you. It'll be all right." But did love conquer all? Could love conquer the theft of a child?

It will never be all right, she thought.

She did not turn on the lights. The room was entirely dark except for the faint-blue glow from the digital clock. Yet she knew every object in the room; everything around her was normal. She did not feel kidnapped. She felt chosen. Adopted. Needed so desperately by Frank and Miranda that perhaps they didn't even know what they'd done to acquire a second daughter. Temporary insanity.

But if it came out, thought Janie, it would be permanent insanity. For all of us.

New Jersey must vanish. Jennie Spring must never be.

She resolved to be Janie Johnson with all her heart, mind, and soul.

She fell asleep feeling better but the dreams

came again, and this time they were of falling. Bottomless falls. Evil below. Evil above. When she woke up, she was hanging on to the pillow with a grip so tight she had ripped the lace trim off the pillowcase. She went silently into the guest room and retrieved more pillows, which she arranged around herself in bed like walls. Huddled in a white percale fortress, she managed to sleep a couple of hours.

In the morning, breakfast was desperate and silent.

Her mother drove her to school, as if Janie might escape otherwise. "Mom," said Janie. "I promise. Okay?"

Her mother nodded shakily. "I'm staying home," she said. "I've canceled everything. If you need me—if you feel upset—if you think even for a minute about running off again—Janie, promise you'll telephone me." It was cold with the beginning of winter and the car heater had not yet begun to warm the car, but her mother was perspiring. She looked as exhausted as if she had just mowed several acres of lawn with a push mower. She looked old.

"I promise," said Janie. "But I'm not going anywhere except class. Today's your hospital day. Go to the hospital."

"It's my tutoring day."

"Then tutor."

"I don't want to tutor."

They giggled. "We sound like two-year-olds slugging it out," said Janie.

Her mother took Janie's hand, turning it over, examining it, as if she might never see the hand again and needed to memorize the texture and shape.

"Mom!" said Janie. "I promise."

"Okay."

"Okay. Have a good day." Janie bolted before either of them broke down.

"Earth to Jane Elizabeth Johnson, Earth to Jane Elizabeth Johnson!" trilled Sarah-Charlotte. She was elegant today: long knit skirt, heavy blouse with a wide dramatic belt, and long coppery earrings that reached her narrow shoulders.

Janie felt at least five years younger than Sarah-Charlotte. "I'm right here," she said. "Stop making a spectacle of yourself."

"I beg your pardon," said Sarah-Charlotte frostily. "You are the one acting crazy."

"What do you mean by that?" Janie tried to occupy herself unfolding a paper napkin for lunch.

"I mean you are out in space today. What's going on in your life that you aren't telling me about? I resent this, Janie. I mean it. What aren't you sharing with me? There is nothing in your life that you are allowed to keep private." Sarah-Charlotte took Janie's napkin away. Janie said nothing. In a more irritable, more honest voice, Sarah-Charlotte added, "Your mother and father telephoned four times yesterday looking for you. Now where were you? What was going on? I can't stand it that you didn't tell me."

"She's in love," guessed Katrina.

Automatically Janie's eyes flew across the cafeteria to locate Reeve.

Every other kid peered or stood to see where she was looking.

"It's Reeve!" said Jason. "I knew it. The old boy-next-door trick."

Reeve waved at her.

"You toad," said Sarah-Charlotte. "You've been doing stuff with Reeve and you didn't call me up and tell me. Our friendship is over, Janie."

A strange, flighty mood was keeping Janie aloft. "That's okay," teased Janie. "I have a replacement over there in the senior section." She felt truly strung out, as if she were a rubber band being stretched, vibrating with pressure.

"Blow him a kiss, Janie," said Adair. "Let's get this romance on the road."

Janie blew Reeve a kiss.

Reeve blew one back.

"Okay, I'm begging," said Sarah-Charlotte. "We're still best friends. Now I want details. All of them."

Jason, Pete, Katrina, Adair, and Sarah-Charlotte swiveled their heads in unison and leaned forward into Janie's face. "You may have my overcooked mushy canned peas if you tell," offered Jason.

"You can have the bottom half of my biscuit, too," said Adair. "It's hardly burned at all. It's supposed to be black like that."

Taking her thick auburn hair with both hands, Janie stacked it in a huge mop on top of her head. She waved her hair at them and said pertly,

"No," and they all giggled. Sarah-Charlotte discussed her belt instead and where she had found it and how many shops she had been to before finding the perfect one, and what the earrings had cost.

After lunch a sick heaviness settled where the silliness had been. Janie's head began pounding. When she tried to swallow, nothing happened. Her throat thickened and went dry.

Fifth-period history the teacher passed out a list of permitted choices for the winter term project. Sarah-Charlotte said in a high-pitched, British *Masterpiece Theater* voice, "Shall I look into changing world opinion on the dropping of atom bombs on Japan, my dears, or shall I examine the personalities of Soviet leaders from Stalin to Gorbachev? I feel slightly faint from the excitement of it all."

The teacher ignored Sarah-Charlotte and sent them all to the library. "You're to do preliminary research. Read articles on subjects that interest you so that you may make an informed decision about a topic you will be investigating for many weeks."

The class charged to the library. "From the pace we're setting," observed Sarah-Charlotte, "you would think we actually wanted to do this."

The librarian, Mr. Yampolski, was everyone's best buddy. He never gave detention to boys who stood on the library tables using newspapers for wings while they played Superman. He never yelled at people who had forgotten how to use the card catalog. He never suggested you should peruse

The Wall Street Journal when what you wanted to do was look at the movie stars in *Teen* magazine. "Hey, Janie, babe," he said. "How's Mom?"

"She's great. Probably can't wait till next summer so she can help you with inventory again." How plausible I sound, thought Janie. Perhaps I will get used to lying, and it will turn real, the way my parents' lies have turned real for them.

"Listen, inventory's the light of my life since your mother started doing it with me. So what's the term paper, kid? Lay it on me. Let's get your reference books out here."

Mr. Yampolski was always twice as excited about your project as you were; if you were fascinated by cowboys, he'd be sure to locate a book about cowboys in Argentina or a *National Geographic* article about cowboys in the Ukraine, and then he'd want to sit with you and exclaim over the pictures. There was nothing Mr. Yampolski enjoyed more than sharing knowledge.

"We're here to look at the prom issue of *Seventeen*," said Sarah-Charlotte.

Even Mr. Yampolski might have argued with that, but too many classes were pouring into the library for him to fight her.

"Why the prom issue?" said Janie. "It's only November."

"You're bound to be going to the senior prom with Reeve," said Sarah-Charlotte.

"He hasn't asked me."

"Of course he hasn't asked you. Boys never think farther ahead than the next meal. But you have to plan, Janie. Especially with your red hair.

You can't wear just any color. Now what do you think of this white gown?"

"Too wedding-y," said Adair, turning the page immediately.

"I hate sharing anything," said Sarah-Charlotte. "Especially magazines. When you hold it, I can't see, Adair. Let's get all the prom issues going back as many years as the library has. Then I won't be subjected to all this sharing. Mr. Yampolski!" she yelled.

"Sarah-Charlotte!" he yelled back.

"Do we have back issues of *Seventeen*?" she yelled.

"Why doesn't anybody ever want my back issues of *The New York Times*?" he yelled.

"Because nobody cares about garbage strikes in New Jersey!" yelled Sarah-Charlotte, triumphant.

Seventeen lay open to a particularly repulsive dress, with layers of tacky lime-green ruffles and ribbon trim. The words "New Jersey" paralyzed Janie momentarily. She felt that the whole room had turned around and was pointing at her, silent mouths shouting, "You, you, you!" the way they would for fouls at basketball games. "*The New York Times* covers New Jersey?" Janie said. Her heart was pounding so hard she could actually see the vibrations of her blouse. "I thought it was for New York City."

"You're so ignorant, Janie," observed Adair. "And no, you cannot appear in public in a neon-green dress. Turn the page."

"*The New York Times* covers the world, my dear," said Mr. Yampolski. "With special emphasis on news events of the greater metropolitan area of New York."

A thin, wispy shudder ran through Janie, like a little snake tunneling. Kidnappings are news events, she thought. "How many years do we have?"

"Twenty. Microfilmed. Want some? I'm offering an especially good price today."

"We'd rather have a good price on a prom dress," said Sarah-Charlotte.

Soviet leaders were bound to have been doing something twelve years ago. Janie walked up to her history teacher and asked to do Stalin through Gorbachev. He was truly thrilled, as if this request meant that teaching was worthwhile after all. Janie felt guilty. She would have to do an extra-good job on the term paper now or he would suspect something. But there was no way she would look up New Jersey here at school, where Mr. Yampolski would read over her shoulder, soaking up knowledge along with her.

When the final bell rang, she left the building immediately, climbing on a different bus from the one that went to her street. People spoke to Janie, demanding to know why she was trespassing on their bus, but she did not hear them. She got off at the town library and went inside.

The librarian there showed her how to use the many-volumed index to the *Times*. Showed her how to find the spool of film in its little file drawer, how to thread it in the viewing machine, how to print out the page if she wanted a copy instead of taking notes.

"Thank you," said Janie, waiting for the librarian to leave her alone. She had read somewhere that when doctors told their patients they had cancer and were dying, the patients invariably ended the conversation by saying "thank you." She felt the cancer of madness inside her brain, the demon of her daymares: its little fingernails scraping.

She turned to the index for twelve years ago. Looking over her shoulder to be sure nobody was watching her, she looked up "Spring, Jennie." It was listed. It was real. It had more than one entry. Day after day they had followed the case of the stolen three-year-old.

She walked toward the microfilm drawers as if she were buying dirty magazines. Opening the shallow drawer, she read labels on white boxes until she found the right date, then took her spool of film.

Over by the window a potted tree had grown huge and lofty. Nobody had expected it to flourish in the dry library, but now nobody wanted to cut it back. Leaves hung into the science fiction books and one branch curled over the microfilm viewer. Janie ducked beneath the bright green leaves and sat on the metal stool. She wound the film on the machine, turned on the lights, and watched *The New York Times* appear on the screen. She had thought they would save only the important articles, like what the president was doing, but no: everything was there, from classified ads to fashion photos. She spun the knob, leaping past one day, and into another. It was difficult to focus, confusing to operate.

What if Sarah-Charlotte or Adair comes up behind me and wants to know what I'm doing? she thought.

She was out of breath. Her brain had ballooned into a misshapen thing filled with demons, while her lungs had contracted, like flat tires, and she was suffocating in the library stacks.

And then, quite suddenly, her own picture stared back at her. The same one that had been on the milk carton. *No ransom has been asked for little Jennie Spring,* read the caption. *Hope that the three-year-old wandered away and would be found has diminished as National Guard units give up the search.*

She read about the shopping mall, the lack of clues, the search. She read quotes from neighbors and police. At the bottom of the column, in a different typeface, it said, "Continued on Page 34."

Janie scrolled around to page 34. A three-column photograph appeared on the screen. It was a family portrait: parents, grandparents, and children lined up, babies on laps, smiles on faces.

She closed her eyes. *It's them.* If I look at them, they'll exist. If I read page 34, I'll know their names. They musn't become real. Mother and Daddy are real. I don't want New Jersey to be real.

She kept her eyes closed and fumbled for the light switch. When she had turned off the machine and the page had vanished, she rolled the film back up and put it in its box. She had to hold on to the edge of the table to find sufficient strength to stand up.

Reeve was beside her.

She stared at him, still struggling for breath.

"I followed you," he said. "In my Jeep. I wanted to give you a ride home. I wanted you to ride with me every day. Always. And you got on the bus."

Janie was so aware of his maleness. They had shared nothing except a kiss in the leaves and another on the sidewalk. "Are you in trouble with your parents?"

Reeve rolled his eyes. "My father wanted to know where I got the money for the trip. See, they think the first step in preventing drug abuse is preventing access to money and they knew I didn't have much. So like a jerk I said I charged it all to American Express and my father took the motel receipt out of my wallet."

"Oh, yikes," said Janie. "You don't think they'll tell my parents, do you?"

"They promised not to. They said your mother and father have enough to worry about already."

"Did you tell them we didn't actually do anything?"

"Yes."

"Did they believe you?"

"What do you think?" said Reeve. "Would you believe your seventeen-year-old son if he—"

A body came between them: thick, middle-aged, female. The librarian here was not as understanding about flirtation in the stacks as Mr. Yampolski. In a dry, sarcastic voice she said, "Are we doing a term paper? And if so, may I inquire as to the subject?"

"Cults," said Reeve without missing a beat.

"The Hare Krishna. How they went from being an idealistic organization of peaceable hippies to major-league crime like drugs and kidnapping."

He had said "kidnap" out loud. Janie felt truly endangered, as if somebody would notice—call the police or the FBI or arrest her mother. "Oh, no, Reeve!" she gasped. "Quick, give me a dime! I have to call my mother. I'm not home! She'll be worried. I have to tell her I'm here."

Janie could hardly punch the pay phone buttons to put the call through. What if her mother had already panicked? Already gone to the school—found Janie had not taken her own bus?

"Hello?" said her mother.

"Mommy!" Janie was sick with relief. Lunch threatened to return. "Don't worry. I'm at the library. I'm looking up a term paper. I meant to call you before I came. Sarah-Charlotte says I've been in outer space all day. Were you worried? Are you all right?"

"I'm fine," said her mother.

"Is that true?"

"No, it's a lie. I'm a wreck. And your father's at a soccer game so I couldn't call him to say you were missing again."

"Mommy, I haven't been to a game of his yet. Reeve's here. He'll drive me. I'll meet you at the soccer field, okay?"

CHAPTER
14

Her father's team won the soccer game.

"It was probably because you and Reeve screamed so loud," he said. "That and running up and down the field to follow the action." He was so glad she had attended his game that she was overwhelmed with guilt for not going before. He introduced all his little players to her, and then to Reeve, and the pride in his voice swamped her.

"What's for supper?" said her father when they were all heading for the cars to go home.

"Is that always your primary concern?" teased her mother.

"It sure is high on the list," he said. "Not much but soccer and daughters come ahead of it." He kissed his wife on the mouth to show that she was also ahead of food. He looked younger. The lines weren't as deep as last night.

"Actually we're going out for pizza," said Janie's mother.

Janie, Reeve, and Mr. Johnson raised eyebrows.

Mrs. Johnson felt that fast foods divided the family. She served old-fashioned meals that always deserved the adjective "solid." The pizza was an offering. *See, Janie, we'll even get you the food you want. Anything—just don't leave the way Hannah did.*

They offered me ice cream once, she thought, and I let them buy me off with that, too.

She did not know if she could even gag pizza down. But there was more to swallow than pepperoni and mushrooms.

Her parents made it clear that it would be thoughtful of Reeve to go on home. He left reluctantly, after Mrs. Johnson agreed that Janie could ride to school with him in the morning. The Johnsons drove to Pizza Hut, making silly, flippant conversation about soccer and Janie's love life.

When the waitress had brought a pitcher of Coke to the table and they were back from the salad bar, her mother said, "I've arranged family counseling at the Adolescent Trauma Center."

"I won't go," Janie said immediately. "I want to think things out for myself." She was already protecting herself from the penetrating eyes of friends and parents. Now she had to keep her lies going in front of psychiatrists who specialized in adolescent trauma?

"I don't want to go either," said her father. "I hate talking about personal things to strangers." He shoved half the objects on the table to the far side—salt, Parmesan cheese, Sweet 'N Low—as if pushing away the invasion of their privacy.

"Besides," added Janie, "we're doing fine."

A complete untruth.

She would never again be honest with her mother and father. She would carry her milk carton around, photograph down. She would lie. She who had never had secrets would carry New Jersey around like a tray, spread in front of her, invisible to all eyes but Reeve's.

Janie stared at her father, trying to imagine him going to New Jersey to steal a child.

With trembling hands, her mother distributed extra napkins. "I think we could use counseling." Her husband and daughter looked away. "We'd all go," whispered her mother. The whisper gave intensity to the simple words. She sounds as if she's praying, thought Janie. She must have prayed for Hannah.

Memory surfaced.

Janie tried to stomp on it. Her feet actually moved, kicking away the memory. The memory came anyhow. Not a daymare. More like a sound track.

She, who lived in a household without religion, knew a prayer.

> *Bless this food*
> *Bless this house*
> *May all my brood*
> *Be quiet as a mouse.*

We recited that at dinner. There were so many of us and we made such a racket. He wanted us to be quiet for just a little while. He . . . my real father . . .

No, no, no, no, no, no!

I want to be Janie Johnson, not Jennie Spring.
Go away! Drop dead! Leave me alone!

"Janie, what are you thinking about?" said her mother.

She surfaced from New Jersey. It was like swimming underwater, having to shake your head before you could see again. "Oh, nothing," she said. The brightness in her voice was so false even the waitress paused and took notice.

Janie tried to do homework.

It was impossible.

She walked around her room, touching, wishing.

On top of a stack of papers lay a small, square, spiral notebook with a silver glitter cover and silver-rimmed pages. Every September, Janie started the new school year by buying an assortment of pretty notebooks from various gift shops. She always intended to write assignments in one, keep a diary in another, copy interesting poems or phrases in a third, and so forth. She rarely made more than a page of entries before the assignment notebook was misplaced or the diary became dull.

She opened the silver notebook. Only two pages had been touched. Janie ripped them out and flipped to the middle, where it looked safe. She began to draft a letter, to help herself think about the unthinkable.

Dear Mr. and Mrs. Spring,

In the school cafeteria I took my friend's milk carton and on it was a photograph of your little girl who was stolen from a shopping center in

New Jersey all those years ago. It was me. I recognized myself. But I knew it could not be true, because I have a wonderful mother and father already, and a wonderful life, and I have always been very happy. So I could not have been kidnapped. It really wasn't me.

She was too tired to write. Her hand shook and the six sides of the pencil hurt her fingers. That's when you know you're weak, she thought. When pencil surfaces wound you. She closed the notebook and put it under the clip in her three-ring notebook along with the milk carton.

In the morning, she fell asleep during math.

During English, when Mr. Brylowe was discussing modern European literature, she opened her silver glitter notebook and wrote again.

Every time I look at that carton I have another memory: of a kitchen and spilled milk, high chairs, and a dog named Honey. A table blessing about mice.

And there's the dress. It's in the attic. Tomorrow when my mother is out of the house I'm going to get it out and iron it. I'll hang it in the back of my own closet where I can see it.

Mr. Brylowe said, "Janie?"

She looked up, startled and unfocused.

"Everybody else has left for lunch, Janie."

The room was entirely empty.

Mr. Brylowe said, "Janie, is there anything you would like to talk about? Anything you'd like to share with me?"

She shook her head.

141

The classroom door seemed terribly far away. Hard to find. And lunch, even though Reeve would be there, hardly seemed worth the effort it would take to reach the cafeteria.

She got halfway there and had to finish her thoughts.

Had to write.

It was like a druggie stabbing his vein.

She stopped right in the hall, holding the silver notebook against the wall for a desk, and writing vertically.

You must promise not to go to the police or even to get mad at my parents. Because they are my parents. They are my mother and father. I love them.

The most terrible thing about this is that I forgot you. I am very sorry. I don't know how or why I could have, but until I saw that photograph of me on the milk carton, I never thought of you.

You can stop worrying. I am all right. I have always been all right. But the thing is, I have not told my parents. I don't know how to tell them that they were part of kidnapping me. I haven't decided yet whether I want to meet you. I know that sounds awful. But I have a family and I love them and I don't know you.

Three times a week after history she had typing. They were learning to do envelopes. Since they had to use up envelopes anyhow, the class was doing a mailing for Students Against Drunk Driving. Janie had twenty-five to address.

The class was filled with the clicking of key-boards, the moans of students making errors, and the continuous demand for replacement envelopes when somebody goofed up too much to use the old one. Everybody wanted to be using the computers instead of the typewriters because you could correct your errors so much more easily.

The afternoon sun came strong and golden through the windows. Both students and teacher were half-asleep. Janie's own mistakes had nothing to do with the heat of the sun. She kept putting her own return address on the envelope instead of SADD's. But the envelopes were still perfectly useful, so she stuck them under the clip-board in her blue-cloth notebook.

For the hundredth time she checked both sides of her milk carton. It was still her.

I'm like a toddler with my blanket, thought Janie. I can't get very far from my carton. Pretty soon I'll be sucking my thumb again.

After school, Reeve caught her so she couldn't take off for the library. "Or points unknown," he said. "Or Sarah-Charlotte's."

In his Jeep they went to the Scenic Overlook and watched the couples for whom it was a Sexual Overlook.

"I can't," said Janie miserably. "No matter what is happening my mind slides around to New Jersey."

"I wish I could say the same," Reeve said. "No matter what is happening, my mind slides around to you. It's consuming my whole life. I don't even have a life except thinking about you."

She was not sure if he meant thinking about Janie, or thinking about sex with Janie.

They kissed each other, but Janie turned away almost before it began and his lips brushed her disappearing cheek instead. He said, "You're losing weight, aren't you?"

"I'm too nervous to eat."

"Tell me."

"Reeve, I want them not to exist! New Jersey, I mean. I don't want them to be down there. Waiting. I feel as if they're going to pop up somehow and leap into my life and I won't have any choice. I want my parents, not them."

He nodded. His cheek brushed against hers and it was a sensation she had never had before: an unshaven cheek.

"Besides," she whispered, "it makes me realize what a horrible little girl I was. Reeve, I'm so afraid to find out what happened. What if I gave up those brothers and sisters, and the father who shouted blessings, just for an ice cream sundae?"

He said, "I suppose you did, Janie. Maybe it was pretty neat to be the center of all that attention. Driving fast and laughing and singing and having ice cream, and new parents and new clothes and a new bedroom."

"I would have been three and a half," cried Janie. "Kids that old know how to use the telephone. They have their phone numbers memorized."

"But would it have occurred to you to call up New Jersey? You wouldn't have felt kidnapped.

144

You were having lots of fun. When they said, 'Pretend you're our little girl'—gosh, Janie, you'd be great at that. You always have some fantasy running in your head. Like that whole Denim and Lace thing."

"I never told you about Denim and Lace," said Janie, embarrassed.

"No, but Sarah-Charlotte did."

"You talked about me last year to Sarah-Charlotte?"

"Yeah. Now do you feel like kissing me?"

She did.

They did.

And it was good. "I love you, Reeve," she said. How easily it came out. How true it was.

"Maybe they were mean to you in New Jersey," suggested Reeve.

"No," said Janie. "I can remember that much. Nobody was ever mean. You know, in a way I'd like to go to that Adolescent Trauma thing and ask a doctor about memory loss. How come I didn't remember?"

Reeve said, "I don't suppose you needed to remember before. Everything was fine. If you hadn't seen the milk carton, it would still be fine."

"I hate that dairy. I'm never drinking Flower Dairy milk again."

"Good. Because you have a milk allergy."

They leaned on each other, snuggling for the best fit. Janie thought that nothing could be nicer than getting comfortable on Reeve's chest. She was aware of his scents: Reeve himself, the faint soapiness of his shirt, a slight perfume from his shampoo.

If it hadn't happened, she thought, I would not be me. I would be somebody else entirely.

It horrified her that she had once daydreamed of being somebody other than Janie Johnson. Jayyne Jonstone, indeed. How precious her own name and address seemed now.

Reeve had supper with the Johnsons. Nobody discussed Hannah or grandparents or the skipped day of school. After dessert (Reeve had Janie's as well as his own; Janie's mother did not seem to see how little Janie ate) they studied together. Reeve was done in three minutes and wanted to know what he was supposed to do for the next two hours.

That night, along with checking her milk carton, Janie checked her SADD envelope, where her real address was so professionally typed. It seemed to her that they might offset each other: the carton and the envelope.

Soccer season was nearly over. Cake decorating was drawing to a close, and her mother wanted to take pottery next.

Janie had taken the polka-dot dress out of the trunk, washed and ironed it, and hung it in the back of her closet. Every morning and every night she touched it, as routinely as she brushed her teeth. She had made dozens of entries in the silver notebook. Writing cleansed: it removed the badness from her mind and kept it safely on the paper.

Autumn had all but vanished. One maple hung on to a few yellow leaves, and a hedgerow was wine red behind the house. On Saturday the sky was indigo blue: like new jeans. The wind was soft and warm, as if it had news to spread.

"Let's go for a drive," said Reeve, who was having breakfast with the Johnsons. He liked breakfast there on weekends because Mrs. Johnson, who ignored weekday breakfast, got excited on

Saturdays and produced waffles, bacon, and melon slices. Reeve's mother just said she had been making breakfast for twenty-seven years and anybody who wanted breakfast again this year knew where the cereal was.

"It's perfect weather to head into the horizon," said Janie's mother, looking out the window.

"It's funny how you feel that tug only in the fall," said her father. "No other season. In the autumn you want to go. Drive. Have a journey."

When had Hannah decided to leave? Janie wondered. Out loud she said, "Where shall we go, Reeve?"

"Anywhere. I have a full tank of gas and I earned money last week cleaning out the McKays' garage and cellar. I'm rich. We can eat lunch anywhere." He grinned at her.

Friday when she got home, Janie had dumped her book bag on the kitchen floor. Now, getting up for more orange juice, she shoved it out of the way and the books fell out, spreading across the linoleum.

"Janie," said her mother crossly, "how many times do I have to tell you to carry your book bag directly up to your bedroom?"

"Six million," said Janie.

With his shoes, Reeve pushed the books into a pile to pick up.

"Reeve," said Janie, "how many times do I have to tell you to handle school property carefully?"

"Six million," he said. "Thanks for the waffles, Mrs. Johnson. Maybe Janie and I will drive to

Vermont and get you more maple syrup." Together he and Mrs. Johnson began picking up the books.

"Vermont!" said Janie's father. "That's four hours away."

"We'd still get back before dark," said Reeve.

Janie's mother scooped up the books nearest her chair. The load was too heavy for her hand and dropped back on the floor. The blue-cloth English notebook fell open.

The milk carton lay exposed.

Janie lunged forward, slamming the cover shut, grabbing her books.

Her parents stared at her.

"Sorry," said Janie with a bright, crazy smile on her face. Her heart was throbbing, her horrible headache had begun again. She already knew tonight's nightmare: the carton falling out, her parents seeing it, New Jersey exposed and waiting.

She put the books back in the book bag, zipped it shut, and ran upstairs with it. Clattering back down, she grabbed the jacket Reeve tossed and slipped her arms in the heavy sleeves. "Let's go, Reeve."

"Telephone if you're going to be out after dark," said her father.

Reeve promised. He took Janie's hand and swung her around like a dance partner. They ran out of the house.

He was in a great mood. He talked steadily. Janie loved to listen to him. In Reeve's childhood, Megan, Lizzie, and Todd had done all the talking. Reeve's delight when at last both sisters and his brother were away came through in his speech: for a change, Reeve could have the audience.

I must have wanted an audience, too, thought Janie. I was only three and a half and I wanted a bigger audience.

Reeve did all the driving. She had not had another driving lesson with either parent. They would have to talk about licenses if they did, and the birth certificate problem, and she was afraid of screaming, "But I know my real birthday! I can make one phone call and they'll send me my real birth certificate!"

She was trying to fence off all the dangerous places, where things might cave in, where they would know that she knew. She kept having the sense that if she could steer her life right, the way Reeve was steering the Jeep right, they would avoid ever hitting the kidnapping.

"I looked up the kidnapping in *The New York Times*," said Janie.

She had interrupted him. Reeve stopped his story and drove on, looking straight ahead, his body stiff.

He thought my mind was on him, Janie thought, and now he knows it wasn't. "I'm sorry. What were you saying?"

He shrugged. "I thought you were going to stop worrying about New Jersey," he said.

"I was."

"So what happened?"

"I can't."

He said, trying to be lighthearted, "I'm not enough distraction for you, huh?"

The only thing anybody wants is to be the center of a universe, she thought. Reeve had to wait for Megan, Lizzie, and Todd to go away before he could be the center. I wanted the center so much I traded my family for an ice cream sundae. She said, "You're not a distraction. You're the light of my life."

She thought he would make a face at this Valentine's-card sentiment, but he said, "Really?" His face relaxed somewhat.

"Really," said Janie. His face relaxed completely.

Reeve stopped at a restaurant. It was too early to eat anything when they were still waffle-stuffed. He ordered Cokes. Reeve chewed ice.

"Don't do that," she said, "you might crack your teeth."

"There are parts of me I wish you'd pay more attention to than my teeth," said Reeve.

They flirted.

She loved the silly sentences, the innuendo. Sarah-Charlotte may look older and act older, thought Janie happily, but I'm the one doing older things.

When Reeve paid for the Cokes, she studied him. How he enjoyed looking in his wallet, seeing the thick wad of money, leaving a generous tip because he was glad to be driving away instead of waiting table. He liked getting her jacket from the peg where he had hung it up, and he liked holding her hand as they left.

I love you, she thought, and she kissed him

151

just as they were going through the doors, so she got caught in the glass, bumping into a patron trying to enter.

If New Jersey hadn't happened, thought Janie, I wouldn't have my own parents or my house or school or Sarah-Charlotte . . . or Reeve.

They never reached Vermont.

They saw a sign for a state park and drove in. A narrow road wound among thick, dark hemlocks and emerged at a cascading waterfall where boulders were surrounded by mountain laurel. The sun glittered on the leaping water, and when they parked, the sun's rays turned the interior of the car into a heated sunroom.

"I love you, Reeve," she whispered, lying against him. "You know what?"

"What?"

"If I ever get in touch with New Jersey, I'll have to say, 'Luckily for me, I got kidnapped.' Of course, I'm not getting in touch. I never think about it anymore. I wrote it all down and spiraled it away."

Reeve took a very deep breath. She giggled when his chest lifted her like an escalator and then sank her back down.

"I called my sister," he said. "Lizzie."

Janie snuggled under Reeve's throat and felt it vibrate when he spoke.

"I told Lizzie everything," said Reeve.

"You what?" screamed Janie. She flung herself backward. She would have thrown things if there had been anything loose in the Jeep.

"I had to, Janie. You need advice. And what do I know? She's a lawyer. Or she's going to be."

"How dare you?" screamed Janie. "How dare you tell anybody without my permission. I haven't even told my own mother and father and here you are telling Lizzie, who I can't even stand!" She was so frantic the Jeep was rocking.

Reeve put on the parking brake. "Listen, Janie, I told her everything you told me and she said—"

"Whatever Lizzie said, I don't want to hear it. I'm sorting this out in my own mind and—"

"You're losing your own mind, Janie."

His voice was so soft she could hardly hear it. Inside her head was a terrible racket: the crying and laughing of the voices of the past. She felt like a snow flurry: she was coming down fast, in tiny wind-whipped particles. "No, I'm not losing my mind," she said desperately. "Am I?"

He held her again. She did not feel like a person in his arms but like a small, scared animal. That word for Hannah's chosen husband, a *mate*, like an animal. Am I really Hannah's daughter? Could that be the truth? Will I turn out weird like Hannah? Am I already weird?

"Lizzie looked up the kidnapping in *The New York Times*, too, Janie, all the subsequent articles and all the follow-ups. Janie, are you ready for this?"

"I'm not ready for anything."

"Lizzie thinks it's Hannah who kidnapped you. We all agree that Mr. and Mrs. Johnson just wouldn't do that. Couldn't do that. Isn't it much more reasonable that Hannah really did run away from the cult? Stopped at that shopping center in

New Jersey? Maybe she had stolen a car or the cult guards had nearly caught up to her. She was afraid. She ran inside and there was this sweet little girl who would hold her hand. Lizzie thinks maybe Hannah took you along for company. And Hannah was such a lost soul maybe she didn't even know she was kidnapping you. But if she did know, she sure wouldn't tell her mother and father when she got to their house."

Peace settled on Janie. She felt heavier, as if her weight might press on Reeve till his ribs broke. She said, "Mother and Daddy aren't bad, then."

"Well, we don't know anything for sure. But that way, your parents' story is entirely true. Lizzie and I can't believe they would have been part of anything criminal or evil."

"Hannah was the evil criminal." Janie was so lethargic she could not imagine moving again. How wonderful to place the crime on a woman who no longer counted in anybody's life.

The sun fondled her lovingly. Or was it Reeve?

In an odd way, she felt even more like an animal: soaking up the sun, no worries, no cares, no concern for the future: just affection and warmth.

"I don't know," said Reeve. "I don't think Hannah sounds evil or criminal. I think she sounds like a scared, cult-blinded automaton. Even at three you were a hand to hold, somebody to talk to in the car, somebody to give Hannah courage until she reached her own mommy and daddy and was safe again."

Janie liked it. It meant that her parents had told no lies. Were sane and good. Really did consider themselves her grandparents. Or parents. "There are too many parents in this," she said to Reeve.

"Tell me about it. And now I've thrown in Lizzie, who is tougher than any four parents anyhow. Lizzie sees kind of a problem, though, Janie. If we tell anybody about it, see. Kidnapping is a federal offense no matter how many years have gone by. Like murder. You can still be tried. So if we say anything at all, the FBI would have to locate Hannah. To prove or disprove our theory."

It took too much effort even to lean on Reeve's chest. She managed to lie down, her head in his lap, her feet on the passenger seat, her back full of gear shifts.

"Isn't that uncomfortable?" said Reeve.

"Yes, but I'm too tired to sit up."

Reeve reached awkwardly into the backseat and retrieved a stadium blanket. "Let's sit out there by the waterfall." He had to uncurl her from the gear sticks. They staggered into a spot of sunshine and he spread the blanket on a rock hot with sun.

"Can you imagine the publicity?" said Janie. "All those horrible newspapers in grocery store racks. Talk shows where everybody else on it has trans-bi-cross sexual habits." She shuddered. "I can hardly wait to be among them."

Reeve said, "I'd settle for any sexual habit at all, Janie."

"I want to finish this topic first."

Reeve sighed. "Lizzie says if you're going to get in touch with New Jersey, you'll have to handle it privately."

"I suppose Lizzie thinks she's the best person in the world to handle it."

"Lizzie has always thought she's the best person in the world to handle anything," said Reeve.

"I've never liked that trait."

"It's even worse when you have to live with it. And when Megan and Todd are exactly the same."

"You know Megan and Lizzie and Todd," said Janie. "You grew up with them. I didn't grow up with my brothers and sisters. Do you think they ever talk about me at supper? Or keep my picture on the wall? Or say to each other—she'd be a sophomore in high school now?"

"I'm sure they do," said Reeve. He was kissing her everywhere. He had unbuttoned nothing, was feeling through the fabric. His mind was definitely not on New Jersey.

"One bad thing is still true though," said Janie, starting to cry.

"What?" He kissed her tears and she kissed his lips, tasting the salt of her own weeping.

"I'm still a rotten little kid who wanted more attention and was willing to be kidnapped to get it."

Reeve laughed. "You can't have been too rotten if they're advertising on milk cartons to get you back."

We're both frantic, she thought. His heart is

racing for me. My heart is racing for fear. She said, "There are only two choices."

"Right. Either we do it or we don't. I vote we do it."

"Wrong. Either I get in touch with New Jersey or I don't. I vote I don't."

"I vote that, too. Who needs another family?" Reeve shifted half on top of her. His weight was warm and convincing.

CHAPTER
16

The following Saturday they rented movies.

Sarah-Charlotte brought Jason and the potato chips. "He's kind of a potato chip himself," she whispered to Janie.

"Hush," said Janie, "I like Jason."

"I do, too," said Sarah-Charlotte, "but he isn't romantic. He's just Jason."

Janie nodded. "I got the romantic in the crowd," she said. "See my little pumpkin pin? Reeve gave it to me on Thanksgiving Day."

"That's so neat!" cried Sarah-Charlotte.

Mrs. Johnson brought in an immense bowl of popcorn.

The four of them sat in a circle on the rug arguing whether the popcorn or the Trivial Pursuit board deserved the middle. Jason said since he had rented the movies, he got to choose the first one. Reeve said somebody would have to sit with his back to the movie if they were playing Trivial Pursuit at the same time, and it wasn't going to be him.

"Bets on who will win Trivial Pursuit," said Sarah-Charlotte, inelegantly stuffing a fistful of popcorn in her mouth.

"Not me," said Reeve. "I never know anything except Sports."

"Not me," said Janie, "I never know anything."

"Oh, good," said Sarah-Charlotte, "I love playing with dumbos. I always know everything. Your go, Janie."

Janie rolled the dice and chose Geography.

Sarah-Charlotte took a card and read the question. "Did Reeve give you the milk carton as well as the pumpkin pin? Does the carton have some sort of romantic significance?"

Janie choked on her popcorn. Reeve slapped her on the back. "Sarah-Charlotte, read the real question."

"But we're all dying to know, Janie," said Jason. "You open your notebook twenty times a day and stare down into that milk carton. Come on, admit it. What's it all about?"

Her mother brought in a platter of turkey sandwiches on rye and two liters of Coke. "I wondered about that, too, darling," she said. "That Saturday you practically had a heart attack because your notebook fell open. All I saw was 'Flower Dairy.' "

Sick fear enveloped Janie like fog. Not here, she thought. Not in front of Jason and Sarah-Charlotte. Not when Mom is the happy hostess and good mother. In fact, not ever. I voted not to have New Jersey.

"Since when is it anybody's business but ours?"

said Reeve. He rolled over against Janie, and kept rolling until he had flattened her. From beneath him she made strangling, let-me-have-air noises.

"Uncle," whispered Janie.

Reeve rolled off onto the carpet again. He lay on his back and said to the rest, "Young lovers deserve privacy."

Sarah-Charlotte looked twice as interested.

She knows where my carton is, thought Janie. She'll study that till she's figured everything out. "Back in a minute!" Janie cried. She ran upstairs into her room, ripped the carton out of the notebook, and rushed into the bathroom. Locking the door behind her, she started to shred the carton to flush it down the toilet.

But she could not tear herself in half.

The milk carton was all that existed of herself.

She walked back into her bedroom and slid it between the mattress and the bedsprings instead.

There had been a week of peace. A solid week without nightmares or daymares.

In the silver notebook Janie wrote all theories and all possible variations. Then she began condensing and choosing the most likely for final drafts.

"What do you want a final draft for?" said Reeve irritably. "What's the plan now? You're going to mail some anonymous notebook to New Jersey?" He was very tense with her. He had taken her twenty miles to go to a very popular, expensive pizza/video place and had bought dozens of tokens. They were sitting together playing a war game, and he wanted to laugh and be silly and win. New Jersey was interfering.

"Of course not," said Janie. "It's just for me."

Reeve said, "It's Pandora's box, isn't it? The myth. The minute you opened that milk carton, it was all there: every evil thing. And you'll never be able to put it back. It's out now."

"The only evil," she said, "is that I don't mind that it happened. I like my life. You see—"

"I can't tell you how tired I am of New Jersey."

"I just want to finish my thought, okay?"

He looked at the screen. He counted the tokens in his palm. He shrugged. "Okay."

She stabbed a game button. "I'm gonna beat the pants off you, boy."

He laughed. "Any time, girl." His bombers attacked her tanks.

She continued her thoughts in the silver notebook. If Reeve was tired of New Jersey, the notebook was all she had now.

Why didn't Frank and Miranda see the newspaper coverage of the kidnapping? It was on the television news for days, too. I suppose they were pretty distracted that week. Hannah returned, complete with granddaughter, and they fled—who had time for a morning paper?

If they had bought a paper the day after Hannah came—Frank would have seen the photograph . . . would have called the police himself . . . taken the Spring's little girl home. Hannah would have been imprisoned; the Johnsons' lives—no, back then they were still Javensens—would have been completely different.

161

Grimmer. Emptier.

I would have no memory of the Johnsons instead of no memory of the Springs.

That night she went to an awards banquet at which her father as coach received a trophy. It was a typical banquet meal: gravy, red meat, and wilted salad. Her father even made a little speech, thanking not just his team and the team parents, but his beloved wife and daughter. He wanted Janie to take the trophy for him.

Janie smiled back at her father, tall and perfect. The after-school athlete was an odd match for the dedicated, formal, elegant committeewoman he had married. They smiled at her, and she knew they had forgotten Hannah right then: she was their daughter. She was their love.

She stood up in the banquet hall and hundreds of little soccer players and their parents applauded for Janie, who had done nothing whatsoever. She stood up and a mother nearby whispered, "Look at that wonderful red hair! Isn't she a beautiful child? The Johnsons are so lucky."

They were photographed as a trio. It would be in the sports pages. Her mother whispered, "I'm glad you wore the purple sweater. Nobody believes a redhead looks great in purple until they see you, Janie."

The photographer shouted, "Smile now. Smile everybody."

Janie smiled.

She thought, if I do not tell New Jersey that I am safe, I am *still* the spoiled brat. Still the rotten daughter who didn't care about the family she had left behind.

The only way to be the good daughter is to tell.

They left the banquet to the handshakes of parent after parent, thanking Mr. Johnson for all the hours, all the sportsmanship, all the encouragement, all the positive thinking, he had given their sons and daughters.

That night Janie lay on her bed holding the telephone in her arms like a teddy bear, dialing the 800 number. This time she let it ring.

It rang once.

Twice.

Three times.

They're not home, thought Janie. How can a toll-free 800 number not be home?

Four times.

Adair's parents have each remarried since the divorce. So Adair has four parents. Two mothers, two fathers. It's not so unusual. I can do it, too.

Five.

There was a click. Her heart slammed upward in her chest. The carefully rehearsed sentences vanished from her head. Her mouth was so dry her tongue scraped. *Oh, my God, what have I done?* her head screamed. I've betrayed my mother and father—I—

"You have reached . . . " began a recording.

The voice asked her to leave her name, number, and a brief message after the tone, and they would get back to her. After the tone, Janie hung up.

The phone rang in her arms.

Its shrillness invaded her heart, making her leap from the bed, scattering books to the floor. *They tapped my phone! They're calling back: they've got me.*

"Hi. Sarah-Charlotte," said Sarah-Charlotte, who always spoke as if she were phoning herself.

"Hey, girl, what's up?" said Janie. She was slippery with sweat; she even smelled of fear, and tasted it in her mouth. It was like biting metal.

"You know Reeve's best friend, Michael?"

"Not very well."

"Better than I do. I adore Michael. Do you think you could ask Reeve to ask Michael to ask me out?"

Janie could hardly get through the conversation. She had to plan every sentence, figure ahead the possible answers to possible questions. It was harder than homework.

Sarah-Charlotte babbled on and on about Michael, and boys, and friendships between boys. Usually Janie could pass an hour, even two hours, on these precise topics. "Don't you and Reeve ever do things with Michael? He and Michael used to be inseparable. Isn't Michael always over at Reeve's house?"

Janie struggled to listen. Her mind exploded with loyalties and parents. She could not seem to put Sarah-Charlotte into the framework of her life. She could not figure out the conversation they were having.

"What kind of friendship is it when the only words you say now are yes, no, maybe, and mm-hmm?" said Sarah-Charlotte. "I'm sick of this,

Janie. You aren't any fun anymore. You don't even like any of us anymore."

She tried to find an explanation that did not include New Jersey. "That isn't true," she whispered, but Sarah-Charlotte had already hung up.

Reeve drove straight for the Scenic Overlook. She knew by his driving. It was more physical, more excited.

I want to be a nice person, she thought. I want to be the kind of little girl who would have screamed for help when she got kidnapped. I don't want to be somebody who thought it was neat. But I don't want to be Jennie Spring.

"Reeve, pull over."

"I can't stop here, Janie."

"Pull over."

He yanked the car to the edge of a road that barely had passing room anyway. Behind them a car honked. Janie opened her door, leaned out, and threw up into some unfortunate person's shrubbery.

If I can't write it out of my mind, she thought, I guess my body is going to throw it out instead.

She refused to go home.

Reeve drove to a diner miles away because she refused to go anyplace where people might recognize them. In the bathroom she mopped herself up with paper towels. Her complexion was like kindergarten paste: white and gluey.

Then she dragged Reeve back to the car. She couldn't sit in the diner. People might look at her.

Reeve said, "Janie, I thought you could just forget about it, but obviously that isn't working.

So you have to tell them. You have to talk about it with them."

"No."

"Janie! You are losing it. Literally."

"Fine."

"No, it isn't fine. You've got to have your parents in this with you."

"No, because the minute I do that, I have to trade them in again for another set."

"No, you don't. Nobody would make you."

"That other family—those people in New Jersey —you think I could just call them up and say, I'm fine, so stop worrying and don't bother me, either? They'll be in court, they'll call the FBI, they'll get lawyers. And I"—Janie's voice turned so ragged it no longer sounded human—"I'll have to admit what happened at that shopping center."

"Janie!" shouted Reeve. "What happened was, a pretty blond woman took a pretty little girl for a ride in her car and they had a great time."

"And the little girl never looked back," said Janie. "I hate her. I hate that little girl." She began to cry. The tears made no noise and took no effort, but they burned fiercely, as if they were the acid remains of her horrible deeds.

She wouldn't let Reeve touch her. She wouldn't answer anything he said to her. They went home, finally, Janie crouched against her door, and Reeve driving with a stiff precision.

A mile from home he said, "I'm sick of this. Now tell them."

"No."

"Tell them," said Reeve, his voice hard and loud, "or I'm not seeing you again."

"I'm not ready to tell anybody."

"You're being stupid. Either wise up or I don't want to be bothered."

"Fine!" she said. "Don't be bothered." She jumped out of the Jeep, slamming the door. Her foot caught on a loose pavement brick and she stumbled, blinded by tears. "This is my life we're talking about!" she shouted at him. "And you don't want to be bothered anymore."

Reeve got out of the Jeep more slowly. "Janie," he said.

"Drop dead." She ran in the side door and slammed that, too.

Inside the house, the tears ripped through her with even more force. How could she have done that? Why be mad at Reeve, the only one on her team, the only one who knew?

Her sobs made a racket, ripped out of her lungs even as she tried to choke them down. It brought her mother and father running. "What's the matter?" they cried, enfolding her.

"I broke up with Reeve," she said, praying it was not true.

The following week was bright with pain.

Life flickered in Janie's face like flashbulbs going off.

No matter where she looked, Reeve was there, but he neither looked back nor waved. In the mornings when she got up, he was already gone. She could not bear to take the school bus again— that public declaration: yes, I lost him. Her mother drove her to school every morning. Afternoons Adair dropped her at home unless she took the bus that passed the town library.

You know life is pretty grim if reading about Stalin and Krushchev beats all the other options, thought Janie. She tried to make herself laugh, but nothing in life was amusing.

Five days after her scene in the driveway, Reeve drove home with a senior named Jessica. Janie knew Jessica by sight, a tall, thin, dark girl with very short hair and a brittle smile. She had thought nothing could be more painful than New Jersey.

She was wrong. Reeve's arm around Jessica kept her awake as many hours as New Jersey ever had.

"If that isn't a classic," said Sarah-Charlotte. She was enjoying her role as comforter. It had made them best friends again. Although she was no longer the best friend Janie wanted. I want *Reeve*, she thought.

"Everybody knows," said Sarah-Charlotte, "that Jessica sleeps around. Was that his reason?" She looked intently at Janie. "Did you go all the way with Reeve or not?"

Janie shook her head. They had come close. All that they had done she had loved. Would always cherish. Would never describe to Sarah-Charlotte.

"Clearly," said Sarah-Charlotte, whose knowledge of sexuality came entirely from talk shows, "that's the only thing that mattered to Reeve in the end."

What mattered to Reeve, thought Janie, is what matters to everyone. Being first in somebody's life. I put New Jersey first. He took it for a long time, considering.

During study hall, Janie opened her silver spiral notebook. Losing Reeve had made one thing clear. If she also lost her parents, she would die.

Never, never, could she get through that.

She had condensed the facts and theories of the kidnapping to four pages. She tore them out of her glitter notebook, folded them, and stuffed it all into an envelope under the clip. She missed having the carton there to look at. She licked the stickum and closed the flap. There, she thought. I'm done thinking about it.

She would pin the envelope and the milk carton to the inside of the polka-dot dress and put all three back in the trunk in the attic. That would store the problem for another season.

Later on in the class, feeling spooky, she put the Springs' address on the envelope. *Mr. and Mrs. Jonathan Avery Spring, 114 Highview Avenue.* It made her heart pound to write it. Did I know that address by heart once? she wondered.

She slid the envelope under the clip in her notebook. This afternoon her mother would be tutoring. Plenty of time for a solitary trip to the attic. She would study Hannah's photographs. And then lock the trunk.

She had to sit at lunch with Jason, Sarah-Charlotte, Adair, Katrina, and Peter instead of with Reeve. She felt like the most conspicuous person in the cafeteria. She did not know where to focus her eyes. She wanted to look at Reeve. Only Reeve. Always Reeve. But Reeve was sitting with Jessica. Laughing.

We didn't laugh enough, thought Janie. I haven't had any laughter to spare since the milk carton.

She wondered if she could learn how to laugh again. If there would be a time, living next door to Reeve, when she would smile in an ordinary way at the driver of that Jeep?

Sarah-Charlotte wanted to have a Pity Party for Janie.

"I'll invite only girls," she promised. "Let's see. Adair, Katrina, Jodie, Linda, Hilary. Who else do you want? Should it be a sleep-over? We'll sit around and talk about how rotten boys are and Reeve in particular."

Jodie.

Memory slugged her.

Jodie.

One of my sisters is named Jodie. "I don't want a Pity Party," she said, starting to cry.

Jason and Pete suddenly had to get extra desserts. They fled the table.

"Well, they won't be back," said Adair. "Boys collapse when girls cry."

"That sounds like Shakespeare," said Sarah-Charlotte.

"Embroidery on pillows," agreed Adair.

The bell rang. Janie walked between Adair and Sarah-Charlotte as they battered their way out of the cafeteria and back to English. *Don't let me be in the doorway the same time as Reeve and Jessica,* she thought. *Please.*

One prayer answered. But only one.

English ended.

History poked along.

Passing period following passing period.

Janie went to her last class slowly, not because she was dawdling but because she felt weak. *I haven't eaten in days,* she thought. *Pretty soon my mother won't just have me at adolescent trauma counseling, she'll have me at the anorexia clinic.*

The halls swayed and grew in the middle and clapped their sides against Janie's head. She touched the lockers to steady herself but was knocked from the wall by a bunch of worthless boys. Druggies and scuzzies, all.

I'm a scuzz, too, thought Janie. Tossing out my family like last week's newspaper.

The halls were empty. She did not know how that had happened. A moment ago she had been one among a hundred kids.

She fumbled with her blue English notebook.

She needed to see the carton.

Dimly she remembered the carton was no longer there. It was between the mattress and the box springs.

But her silver notebook was there.

No, it wasn't. It was in her book bag.

But the envelope was still there.

No, it wasn't.

There was nothing under the clip.

The clip was broken.

She had used the clip so often that the cheap little spring had snapped. The envelope was gone.

I addressed it, she thought. To New Jersey. It was one of the SADD mistakes with my real return address on it.

But no stamp.

It can't go anywhere without a stamp.

Unless some Good Samaritan stamped it for me.

Unless the post office delivers it and charges the postage to the Springs.

If it's been mailed, it will be read.

They'll know.

In two days, the Springs will know who I am and where I am.

How am I going to save my mother and father now?

Her thoughts stabbed her separately, knife after knife of fear.

Past the offices, past the school library, past language labs Janie walked. Reeve had last-period chemistry. She found the room and opened the door, walking in. Juniors and seniors looked up, startled. She could not see their faces. Reeve was somewhere among them but her eyes would not focus.

The teacher was writing on the blackboard as he lectured, his back partially to the class.

"Reeve," Janie said, plowing across the room like a tractor.

The teacher turned, chalk in hand. "Uh—miss?" he said.

"Reeve, I need Lizzie's phone number," said Janie, walking steadily toward Reeve, although there were desks and knees in her path.

Reeve unfolded from his desk. Took her shoulder, turned her around. "Be right back," he said to his teacher.

"And just where do you think you're going?" said the teacher.

But they were out of the room and the teacher did not bother to follow them.

"You're pushing me," said Janie.

"I'm walking at a regular speed," said Reeve. "You're trying to walk while standing still. Pick up your feet. Are you on drugs or something?"

"I don't think so. I need Lizzie's phone number. Reeve, you won't believe what I've done. How stupid I've been."

"I think I could believe that," he said.

She talked. He drove her home. "I hate to play psychiatrist with you, but you didn't lose that letter by any accident, Janie. Any more than you wrote it and put it in an envelope and addressed and sealed it by accident. You had to get out of this somehow, and that's the route you took."

The house was empty. They went into the kitchen where Janie stared at the wall phone and Reeve automatically checked her refrigerator for something to eat. It embarrassed him and he shut the door without taking anything.

He wrote down Lizzie's number for her. "Do you want me to call her first?" he said.

She shook her head. She was starting to cry. Now she could see him clearly: Reeve, whom she adored. No wonder he had walked her out of chemistry; she must have looked completely demented, storming desks to get at him. She could imagine the class snickering. Telling Jessica. Preparing to humiliate Reeve when he got back.

His fingers, full of car keys, rested stiffly on the counter. She would have to give him permission to go. Reeve would force himself to be neighborly to the end. She bit the insides of her cheeks. She did not want to blackmail him by crying. "Thank you for the ride home," she whispered. "You don't have to stay."

The empty house seemed very noisy. The freezer

hummed. The furnace buzzed. The clock ticked. Her own pulse throbbed in her forehead. She managed to look at Reeve.

"Janie," he said, "I'm sorry."

She nodded behind the blind windshield of her tears. "Me, too. It's okay." She turned away from him. Think about Lizzie, she ordered herself. One disaster at a time. Think how you're going to beg Lizzie to call New Jersey before they get the letter and call the police.

"No," said Reeve, swallowing audibly. "I mean, I'm sorry and I want to make up. That kind of sorry."

CHAPTER
18

In their place," said Janie's father, "I'd move heaven and earth to ruin the people responsible."

Lizzie sat quietly, having laid out the circumstances so easily, so clearly, that Janie marveled. It had taken Janie weeks of daymares to work her way to the end of this; Lizzie reached the end in ten minutes. Lizzie's green wool dress had a narrow waist and very full skirt. Sitting primly on the edge of the coffee table, her skirt draped to the carpet, she looked like a tent in which tiny children would want to play house.

"The Springs might understand," said Janie. She was soaring. There was no burden left. She felt like dancing, laughing, throwing confetti. It's over, she thought, dizzy with relief.

"I wouldn't understand," said her father. "I'd have the police and the FBI, SWAT teams and old college roommates, all surrounding this house to get *my* daughter back." His hands knotted into fists, as if he, too, would gladly have a fight with somebody; anybody.

"Can't you imagine the SWAT teams surrounding the house?" said Reeve, starting to laugh.

"Unfortunately, yes," said Janie's father.

Janie and Reeve began giggling, acting out SWAT teams with submachine guns peering in their windows. "You know what?" said Janie.

"What?"

"I am starving. I haven't eaten in two weeks, I've been so nervous. I could eat my shoelaces. What is there to eat, Mom?"

"Let's order a pizza," said Reeve.

"Especially when you talk like that," said Janie's father, "you feel like my daughter. Food first." His control broke; tears suddenly made little gleaming rivers on his face, like gold in rocks. He put his arms around Janie. "Hannah would have faded away under this much stress."

"I thought about it," said Janie, "but I reconsidered. I'm tough." She gave her parents an impish grin. "I was well brought up."

Her father managed half a smile. "What am I going to say to those parents?"

"Maybe they'll be nice about it," said Janie.

"Maybe they won't," said her mother. On her mother's lap lay the flattened milk carton. The stolen child who was Jennie Spring, who was Janie, smiled back over the years.

I don't need to see it again, thought Janie. It's over. I'm safe.

Reeve said, "Pepperoni? Mushrooms? Sausage?"

The telephone rang.

Everyone but Lizzie jumped. Shrill rings penetrated their hearts, like surgery. Nobody crossed the room to answer it.

"Probably my mother wondering where I am," said Reeve, but he looked white and afraid of the phone.

"Sarah-Charlotte," said Janie. "She's mad at me."

Her mother's laugh quivered. It was not really a laugh at all; it was a splintered soul. My nightmares laughed like that, thought Janie. "Or New Jersey," said her mother.

The phone rang eleven times. A determined caller. Janie's mother had one hand on her mouth, the other on her throat, as if to contain her fears.

"Getting worked up," said Lizzie, "is not going to help us design our approach."

"Lizzie, have you ever been worked up over anything in your life?" said Reeve.

Lizzie ignored him. He was merely a pesky baby brother. She said, "We have the weekend. They can't possibly get the letter before Monday."

Janie's mother said, "I can't believe this is my life."

Lizzie waited two seconds to pay tribute to this sort of emotionalism and then continued, "But as long as the situation has arrived, Janie, we should deal with it. I'll call the Springs."

"Wait a minute," said Janie's father. "I would take bets that the letter didn't get mailed. The more logical assumption is that it's in the trash at the high school. The janitors swept it up with candy wrappers and discarded quizzes. Which means no one in the world knows but us. We don't have to take any action."

Janie's mother raised a haggard face. "Oh,

Frank," she said. "If we don't take any action, then we *have* kidnapped her. We *have* stolen her." Her mother slumped, defeated and afraid.

All I suffered since October, Janie thought, Mom's getting slapped with tonight. "But you are my parents," said Janie. "That's why I didn't do anything. I know who I am. Janie Johnson."

Her mother whispered, "It seemed so logical at the time. Oh, Frank! Frank! Do you think Hannah really did say this was her baby, our granddaughter? Or do you think we decided on that ourselves, because we needed her so much?" She began sobbing uncontrollably, stretching hands toward her husband. The thin fingers of her left hand glittered with her diamond engagement ring, her gold wedding band, the ruby twenty-fifth-anniversary ring. He took the hand with the rings and held it between both of his. He sank to one knee, and his wife, still holding his hands, bent over it. They looked as if they were proposing to each other.

"I'm yours," said Janie desperately. "Don't cry." She was excluded from their pain. She felt as if she had caused it, would always cause it; that while Frank and Miranda were a unit, she had no family now; neither here nor in New Jersey. "Mommy?" said Janie, as if calling her mother back.

Together, dimly, her parents looked up; they were ten years away.

They can remember it, thought Janie. I have found a few scraps of memory, but to them it is bright: the day Hannah brought a little girl to fill their lives.

"Don't be mad," Janie mumbled. "Please don't be mad."

Her mother pulled Janie down onto the chair with her; there was no room; Janie sat on her mother's lap. She had to curl her spine to fit in the soft, safe spot above her mother's breast. When she wept, she could not tell whose tears were on her cheek. "If I could have any wish," whispered her mother, "it would be that no parent on this earth ever suffered a missing child. And I made it happen to another mother."

"Well, if I had any wish," said her father, "it would be to keep Janie."

"You will," said Janie. "I'm not going anywhere."

"The courts and the Springs may have different ideas."

"You could run away again," suggested Reeve. "After all, you know how it's done."

"Reeve," said Janie's father, "you are getting tiresome."

"Sorry."

Janie was faintly surprised that Reeve and Lizzie were still there. It seemed to her that she and her mother and father had gone where no one else could go: some ghastly voyage of past and present, guilt and anger.

"Maybe we should telephone them right now," said her mother. She frowned uncertainly at the chair, as if unsure that any seat could be safe.

"What would you say?" asked Janie. "Hi, this is your stolen daughter's mother, who thought she was her grandmother, who didn't mean this to happen, and please don't get mad at the kidnapper, because she was a lost soul herself and only wanted company while she ran away from *her* kidnappers."

"They'll think we're insane," said Janie's mother. "The Springs are not going to believe that normal people could have gotten themselves into such a grotesque situation. They'll never let you stay with us, Janie."

The discussion had acquired velocity. Janie felt as if she were hurtling, brakeless, toward yet another cliff. "Lizzie will handle it," said Janie loudly. I just got away from the edge, she thought. Don't shove me over again. "Lizzie will tell them to let it go. Stop worrying and let us be."

"Stop worrying?" repeated her mother. "Do you think I have ever stopped worrying about Hannah? Do you think there's been a night in my life when I haven't prayed for her safety? When I haven't wondered if we did the wrong thing, letting her vanish forever? Janie, no mother ever lets go."

"You pray for Hannah?" said Janie, amazed. "You never said you believe in God."

"I have no beliefs," said her mother. "Only hopes. They'll have to meet you, Janie, these Springs. We'll have to meet them."

"No! They aren't real right now. I don't want them to be real. I want them to go away."

"They've waited long enough," said Janie's mother. "I know what it is to lie awake year after year, never knowing what happened to your little girl. I know what it is to cry out on her birthday, *If only, if only!*"

Even Lizzie's eyes were wet.

"Lizzie could meet with them first," said her mother. "We have to protect Hannah. I wonder if they would promise—no, we can't ask that."

"Don't ask, Lizzie. Tell. Tell them either they're nice about it or I won't see them," said Janie.

Lizzie was taking mental notes. "Then you will see them if they agree not to try to find Hannah or prosecute anybody?"

Janie found herself pushing her parents together to make a shield against the enemy. This is how Hannah felt, she thought. The world caved in and she had no hiding place.

"Maybe after Lizzie sees them, it'll be over," said Reeve.

Lizzie's voice was calm and factual. "It'll never be over."

Never over, thought Janie. This isn't a term paper; I won't pass it in. This isn't high school; I won't graduate. *This will never be over.*

Lizzie stood up, the tent of her skirt rearranging itself gracefully; she was lean and elegant and clever. "I'll telephone the Springs. I will arrange Saturday or Sunday for a preliminary meeting. I will suggest to the Springs that the meeting with you, Janie, take place later in the month without your mother and father there."

"I suppose you'd be the best escort," said Janie. She was crushing her mother. She stood up. Her mother stood with her. Her father moved closer. They were like children in a camp race: legs tied together, stumbling to the finish.

"Of course," said Lizzie, who had never had trouble being modest.

"I want to go, too," said Reeve.

"Nonsense," said Lizzie. "What do you think it is, a movie and popcorn? It's going to be very emotional."

Her mother let go and walked shakily to the cherry table where the library books and the Kleenex sat beside a bowl of yellow and blue dried flowers.

"Then I'm not going," said Janie. "I've had enough emotion. I just want this to end happily ever after."

"Not everything does, Janie," said her father. "Hannah didn't. I don't see how this can."

He was so weary it terrified her. So old she was afraid for his life. "It has to!" cried Janie. "Tell the Springs, Lizzie. Tell them it has to end happily ever after."

Her plea echoed in the living room. The deep sofa was just furniture; the scarlet and blue just colors. The room felt no difference; it would be as lovely after Lizzie saw the Springs as before. Reeve was watching Janie sadly. Her father was unfolding a handkerchief to blot his tears. And her mother had not, after all, crossed the room to get a tissue. Slowly, hypnotically, she was dialing the telephone.

"Mommy?" said Janie. She could not catch her breath. "Mommy, who are you calling?" She tried to see the spinning numbers.

Her mother dialed another digit.

"Mommy, are you calling for pizza?"

Her mother dialed beyond seven digits. She was calling long distance. Out of state. *New Jersey.*

"A mother," said her own mother, "would need to hear her baby's voice." Her mother's face was so soaked in tears it might have been raining.

"I'm not Jennie, though," whispered Janie. A split personality, she thought: I am truly two people. I have to choose. A good daughter or a bad one? But I have two sets of parents. How can I be good to both of them?

The dialing ended.

In the velvety silence of the room Janie, Lizzie, Reeve, her mother, and her father listened to the telephone ring in New Jersey.

Was it ringing in the kitchen? Where the twins had sat in high chairs? Where a laughing father had said a homemade blessing? Where a little girl once spilled milk?

The phone rang a second time. A third time.

Happily ever after, thought Janie. *Please be nice people.*

With numb fingers Janie took the phone from her mother. I should have had something to eat, she thought. I'm so hungry I'm dizzy.

It rang once more.

In New Jersey somebody picked up the phone.

"Hello?" said a woman's voice.

Janie clung to her mother. She said, "Hi. It's . . . your daughter. Me. Jennie."

ABOUT THE AUTHOR

CAROLINE B. COONEY is the author of several novels for young adults, including *Family Reunion*, *Camp Girl-Meets-Boy*, *Camp Reunion*, *The Girl Who Invented Romance*, *Among Friends* and *Don't Blame the Music*, an ALA Best Book for Young Adults. She lives in Westbrook, Connecticut.